TANSY

Also by Marie Campbell

The Crows are Crying
ISBN: 0-595-47199-4

iUniverse 2007

TANSY

Marie Campbell

DB

DIADEM BOOKS

Published by Diadem Books

For information, please contact:

Diadem Books
Ocean Surf
CLASHNESSIE
IV27 4JF
Scotland UK

www.diadembooks.com

This is a work of fiction. Characters and situations are entirely a result of the author's imagination.

ISBN: 978-0-9559741-9-9

Ring a Ring of Roses
A Pocket full of Posies
Attischoo Attischoo
We all fall down!

Author's Note

Apologies to Gaelic scholars for the spelling of Donald. It is important for the story. The correct spelling is Domhnall.

Foreword

THE plague had been around for centuries but in 1665 the great plague hit London. It had started off in the poorer areas. The only way they could get rid of rubbish that included human waste was to throw it onto the streets, which became a perfect breeding place for rats that carried the plague. It was one of the hottest summers in memory. As the deaths mounted, panic set in.

The rich people could afford to flee from London but not the poor. King Charles and his court moved to Hampton Court Palace.

The official records of the deaths, though not exactly accurate, was estimated at 100,000 perishing in and around London, although some believed it could be higher. The great fire, which came a year after, cleansed the city but left thousands of people homeless. Many died of cold and hunger.

Two songs mentioned, composed and sung in the 1600's, were 'The Water is Wide' or 'Waly Waly, gin Love be bonny' and 'Nut Brown Maiden'—original authors unknown.

CHAPTER 1

THE old men sat round the fire in the village inn. They had attended the funeral that day of old Sir Michael Howard.

"Aye, he was a proper gentleman," said Seth, one of the old men.

"I reckon he missed his Lady Sophie when she died two years back."

"Seth, you must have known them when they first took over the estate."

"I did that, working as a cattleman, and the missus working in the big house as a cook.

"The estate has been in the Howard family for many generations.

"Lady Sophie had been a bit of a wild lass before meeting Sir Michael. She was an only child. Her parents doted on her. They were wealthy, owning all the lead mines in the area. A rumour had it that Sophie had had a child to some unsavoury lad. She was sent away to have it. The whole thing had been hushed up.

"She married Sir Michael and there was never a happier couple.

"Sophie took a great interest in all the people on the estate.

"They were married for some years and with no sign of a family they decided to adopt. They came home with a little boy, Ralph. He was going on four.

"The missus came home from work one day and told me that Ralph was going to get the estate when Sir Michael died since there was no other family. Then, to everyone's surprise and delight, Lady Sophie fell pregnant and had a baby boy. They called him Michael, the traditional family name of the Howards.

"I remember the celebrations at the big house. My, it was grand! The whole village was so happy for them."

Seth sat puffing his pipe, his mind away in the distant past.

One of the old men nudged Seth.

"Sir Michael must have been happy to have seen his son Michael married."

"Aye, he was that. A lovely lady she is, but mind you, she seems a bit delicate to me, having to manage the big house and all the servants. Kathryn Moran, she was, before marrying Michael, her family as old as Michael's; her people own the woollen mills in the nearby village of Trent.

"It was while visiting her school friend, Katy, at her home at the Gordon's farm which adjoined the Howard's, that she met Michael for the first time..."

♣

Michael and Ralph had gone to Jim Gordon's farm to discuss some of the fencing at the boundary. They were deep in conversation when Kathryn walked towards them. She was carrying a basket of mushrooms.

She smiled at Michael and Ralph and turned to Jim Gordon.

"Just look at what we are having for tea tonight."

"Good lass," said Jim. "Make sure Katy lends a hand."

"Oh, I'm sure she will," she said, her blue eyes sparkling.

Kathryn walked towards the house, her fair hair falling below her neat little waist in the sun. It shone like gold.

Ralph and Michael were silent for most of the way home.

Then Ralph turned to Michael. "I wouldn't mind giving that Kathryn a tumble in the hay."

Michael turned on him, furious. "You can be so uncouth! I know the reputation you have with the young village girls. Just keep your filthy mind away from Kathryn."

Ralph looked at him in surprise. It was the first time good-natured Michael had turned on him.

"My my," he said. "I think you are smitten."

Michael ignored him, and kicked his horse into a gallop. No more was mentioned about the subject—until it all blew up again a few months later at the Harvest Dance.

It always took place in the big barn at the Howard's. There was great excitement all around the farms and the village, for the Harvest Dance, apart from the New Year celebrations, was the biggest event of the year.

The young girls were busy stitching and sewing, most of them too poor to buy new dresses. They were doing up their old ones with new bits of ribbon and lace. Corn Dollies were being made by the young newly married girls as fertility charms.

Even the old farmers took the last sheaf of corn from the field to hang over the door or mantelpiece. It would stay there until the following harvest even though it would be falling to bits. To throw it out was bad luck and could mean a poor harvest following.

The barn was scrubbed and cleaned, the walls whitewashed. Bales of hay were stacked in the corner to be used as seating. Branches of the beech trees and all the trees that had turned into the beautiful red and gold of Autumn were placed in old milk churns around the barn. Large trestle tables were placed ready for all the food, which was provided by the estate. There were large barrels of beer, Elderberry wine, Birch wine and many more wines, most of it made by the locals the year before and left to mature in big store jars. It had been a good harvest.

Everyone was in high spirits the night of the dance, a beautiful clear night with a touch of frost. A full moon shone as bright as day. The musicians started to play. Kathryn and Katy arrived with Katy's dad and some of the lads from their farm.

Kathryn looked beautiful in a pale blue satin dress that swept to the floor, the skirt sewn with tiny rosebuds, round her shoulders a fine lace wrap.

Katy, too, looked lovely in her dress of pink organsie. Little frills fell from her waist to her ankles. She, too, had a delicate lace wrap round her shoulders.

Katy never wanted to be anything else but a farm girl, sometimes doing a man's work. Her mother had died when she was just a small child. She had been brought up by her father, who she adored. She was broken hearted when he sent her away to school.

Then she met Kathryn who took pity on the lost shy girl. They become firm friends and it was Kathryn who helped her with her dress.

The barn was packed, everyone waiting for Michael and Ralph to arrive. Old Sir Michael was not well enough to attend, otherwise, as tradition dictated, he would have led the dancing.

Michael and Ralph arrived, both looking handsome in their different ways—Michael, tall, fair haired, blue eyed with delicate features, Ralph, dark haired, dark eyed, leaning towards swarthy. He could be charming, one thought, or dangerous.

The music started up, playing a dance..

Michael had noticed Kathryn across the room. Their eyes met. He stepped forward to lead the dance with her.

Ralph pushed him aside and held out his arm to her.

"May I have this dance, Kathryn?"

She had no choice but to lead the dance with him.

There was clapping as they danced around. "You know what this means?" he whispered to her. "Everyone will think we are a couple."

Kathryn stopped dead. "I think not," she said. "Please excuse me." She left him standing in the middle of the floor.

Michael had seen it all happening and walked across.

"Kathryn, will you do me the honour of finishing this dance with me?"

They whirled away, leaving Ralph still standing, a look of fury on his face. After that Michael and Kathryn danced most of the night together.

Looking round, Kathryn spotted Katy dancing with Ralph

"That's a few times they have been up dancing."

"She seems to be enjoying herself," said Michael. "Don't worry about her."

Kathryn flushed with happiness when Michael asked her if he could ride over to the farm the next day to see her.

"Yes, I would like that," she said.

CHAPTER 2

JUST then Katy came running into the barn, tears streaming down her face, her beautiful dress torn and covered in mud. Everyone crowded round her. Kathryn held her close. "What happened, Katy?"

"It was *him*, it was him. He tried to have his way with me! He pushed me onto the ground. He kept saying 'you were brought up on a farm, you know what it's all about'!"

"Who was it Katy? Who was it?" her father was shouting. "I'll kill him!"

"It was Ralph. He asked me to stand at the door to get fresh air. I was feeling so warm. It was so lovely in the moonlight. We walked just a little bit into the yard. The next thing I knew," Katy sobbed, "he was on top of me, pulling at my dress, but I managed to get away."

"Where is he now?" her father was demanding. "Let me get my hands on him!"

"Please father, just take me home."

Her father, white with rage, shouted, "Never again will we set foot on Howard land!"

Michael, just as angry and upset as Katy's father, marched into the house.

Ralph was lolling back in an easy chair, a drink in his hand. "What a to-do! She was asking for it, you know."

Michael made one dive for him and slammed his fist into his face. He continued punching him. God knows where it would have ended because Michael in his rage had the strength of ten men.

Some of the farm workers, checking the livestock before going home, heard the commotion and ran in to separate them.

Michael, still upset, knew that because of Ralph their lifelong neighbours, the Gordons, would no longer be friendly with them. And what was worse for Michael, he would no longer be able to meet Kathryn there.

For days he rode to the boundary fence hoping to see Kathryn and had to put up with the smirk on Ralph's face each time he returned dejected.

Weeks went by and because of the nature of the work on the estate they were forced to work together.

Then one day Michael went to the market in Trent. He was passing the smiddy when he heard laughter. He stopped in his tracks. He would know that laughter anywhere! He looked into the smiddy and there was Kathryn.

The blacksmith was busy shoeing her horse.

"Kathryn," he shouted, "I'm so pleased to see you!"

"I thought I was never going to see you again," Kathryn laughed.

"I don't go to the farm anymore. I feel a bit responsible at what happened to Katy, but she meets me here." Michael was overjoyed. "Can I meet you here as well?"

"Dear Michael, I would love that," Kathryn smiled.

After that they were seen riding about the countryside, so happy together.

Just before Christmas, Michael asked Kathryn to marry him. He visited her parents. They were delighted and the wedding was arranged for the Spring.

Her parents were a bit upset that she wasn't getting married at her own home, but Michael explained that it was his family's tradition that the wedding should take place in the little church on the estate. They understood this and were soon into all the planning for the wedding.

Apart from the work they had to share, Michael saw very little of Ralph, who was off to the village every night after work and was getting quite a reputation with drinking and gambling.

Old Sir Michael was fading fast. Everyone was hoping that he would live to see Michael married. For Sir Michael's sake, knowing it would please him, Michael asked Ralph to be his best man. Michael was surprised when he said yes.

Michael, up and dressed, wandered round the house making sure everything was perfect. The wedding reception was to be held there. Cook had been buying food for weeks, driving all the trades people mad. Everything had to be of the best and she had done well, catering for over a hundred guests.

Michael looked around for Ralph. It was getting close to the time for leaving for the church. There was no sign of him. Nobody had seen him that morning but he had been in the village inn the night before.

Michael, worried that if he didn't leave for the church now, he would be late. He set off hoping that Ralph would be there. When he arrived there it seemed as if the whole village had turned up to see the wedding—but there was no sign of Ralph.

His father was waiting in the porch in his wheelchair, his nurse looking after him. "I just wanted to wait here to welcome you into the church," he smiled.

Michael hugged the frail old body, glad that he was to be there on the most important day of his life. He walked into the church and stood before the altar. Still no Ralph, no best man—and then a thought struck him. No ring! With the sound of the bridal music in his ears, he panicked. Then he felt a gentle tug at his sleeve. His father was beside him. His nurse was taking off his father's wedding ring. He smiled such a beautiful smile at Michael. "I make a good best man," he said in his weak voice.

Just then the organ music sang out and Kathryn walked down the aisle to him. Michael's heart filled with such love and pride at her beauty!

A beam of light shining through a stained glass window bathed her in its light as she walked and gave her an ethereal look.

Ralph appeared the day after the wedding. He offered no explanation about his absence and Michael never asked him. He was too worried about his father who was growing weaker every day and three days after the wedding he died.

Ralph sat on the hillside after the funeral, looking down at the house. It was a huge building built in an L-shape with a turret at the end of each gable. It had been built solidly in grey granite. It had stood there since the first Howard built it more than three hundred years before.

His anger and jealousy knew no bounds. 'It should have been *mine*,' he thought. 'If Michael had not been born it *would* have been! Who knows,' he consoled himself, 'it still could be!'—and a black look crept over his face.

CHAPTER 3

I̶T was Autumn, the busiest time on the farm and throughout the Estate.

Ralph still went out at night, coming home in the early hours. He had gathered some unsavoury characters around him. The locals kept well clear of them.

It was Michael's job to attend to all the accounts and wages. Lately he was finding there were quite a lot of discrepancies. It had been a good year with the sales of livestock, yet the money was down quite a bit.

When he mentioned this to Ralph, he flew into a rage. "Just what are you accusing me of? I have had to spend a lot of money on repairs to the estate houses. Remember, father had let things go quite a bit." No more was said but Michael wasn't entirely satisfied.

"You are worried, Michael," Kathryn said, putting her arms around him. "I know because when you are, you scratch that birth mark at the back of your neck."

"So the old birthmark gives me away, does it?" Michael laughed.

"It's funny, but father had one in exactly the same place and his father before that."

All had a birthmark shaped like a tiny star.

"Father used to laugh and say that all the Howards were star struck."

Trent village was mostly a farming community where everyone knew everyone. Sometimes extra hands were brought in to help with the harvest, or when there was a big shoot on the Estate extra beaters were brought in.

When the man appeared in the village he was noticed immediately. He was sitting in the seat opposite the inn. He looked like a tramp.

His hair, jet black and greasy, hung onto his shoulders. His clothes, dust stained, looked as though at one time they had been of good quality.

As soon as the inn door opened he got up and went in. A few of the old village men appeared in the inn. One could tell they were regulars at the inn, not so much for drink but for each other's company.

They watched the newcomer with interest. He was counting out a few coins to pay for the drink in the bar. He looked across at the old men.

"Can I join you?" he said.

The old men hesitated for a moment, then one of them pulled out a chair for him.

"Where do you hail from?" one of them asked him.

He looked at the old man with sharp dark eyes.

"I'm from here and there," he said. "But this is where I was born and where I lived till I was twenty years old." He nodded. "Oh aye, I had my fun and games here, then I got a bum's rush from one of your gentry over the way. He was afraid that I was getting too close to his precious daughter Sophie."

The old men glared at him. One of them reached over for him, knocking over his chair. "I don't want to hear another word from you! Lady Sophie was much loved here. She would never have had anything to do with the likes of you."

"Hold on," the man said. "I never said that anything had happened between us. We were both young and enjoyed running about the countryside together. Her father sent her away in case she got too close to me. It was you people in the village who believed she was with child and was sent away to have it. As it happens, a girl in the village was expecting a baby. I was the father. I had got drunk one night and that was when it happened. I would never have gone with her sober. She was a vicious slut. She didn't want the baby and as soon as it was born it was sent to an orphanage. A wee boy, it was. I could do nothing then but I still kept a trace on him. His mother couldn't wait to get her claws into another man. I heard that she had gone to London and had become a pickpocket and while running away from the police she was knocked down and killed by a coach. Good riddance, I say."

He finished his drink.

"Now which one of you fine gentlemen are going to buy me a drink? As you can see I'm a bit short of cash at the moment."

"What do you mean 'at the moment'?" one of the old men said.

"Oh, didn't I tell you? I have made arrangements to visit my son. He landed lucky, adopted by rich people. As I said, I kept a trace on him. Maybe you know him? His name is Ralph—Ralph Howard, and I am going to meet him when I finish this drink you were so kind to buy me."

When he had gone the old men sat in stunned silence, shocked by the story the man had told them.

CHAPTER 4

NOTHING more was heard of the man, but two days later his body was found in the river. It was said that he had tried to cross the river at the deepest part and had fallen and cracked his head. Nobody knew who he was.

A bit strange, the old men thought. Someone born and brought up in the village would have known the river like the back of his hand. Why choose to cross at the deepest part? They shook their heads but said nothing. There was never any mention to anyone of him being Ralph's father.

Kathryn was relieved. Michael and Ralph seemed to be getting on better. Ralph even offered to take on some of the jobs that Michael hated, but now and again Kathryn caught a strange look on his face as he looked at Michael. 'I am being silly,' she thought to herself.

Kathryn and Michael had been married for over three years and it was only now that she felt she belonged. She still met Katy once a week in the village on market day and caught up with all the local news. And it was Katy who told her about the man who had drowned in the river. How strange, she thought. Michael had never mentioned it.

At dinner that night she brought up the subject. Michael looked puzzled.

"I never knew anything about it." He turned to Ralph. "Do you know?" he asked him.

"Well yes," he nodded. "I heard about it. It was only a drunken old tramp."

Michael and Kathryn looked at each other. This was Ralph showing his cold blood and his real nature.

Kathryn, in the middle of a talk with Michael about the estate, suddenly put her hand to her mouth and rushed into the nearest toilet. She was violently sick. She recovered after a minute but still felt a bit shaky.

Michael held her close. "What on earth brought that on? Had you been eating something that disagreed with you?"

She shook her head.

"Right," said Michael. "Bed with you. I'm going to fetch the doctor."

In no time Michael was back, ushering the doctor into the bedroom. After just a few minutes examination he held her hand. He was smiling.

"You, my dear, are going to have a baby. I reckon that you are about three months pregnant. You are young and strong. I don't think there will be any problem. You may suffer bouts of sickness. That is quite usual at the beginning."

When the doctor had gone they clung together, overcome with happiness.

Michael couldn't wait to tell everyone. When he told cook, she sniffed, "I could have told you that—she had all the signs months back."

Michael hugged her, a faithful old servant to him and his father before him. He didn't even know her name. She was always called

16

'cook' since he was a boy. She was married to Seth who was now retired after working all his life on the estate.

Ralph, when told, just nodded.

"Well, congratulations. Now do you think we could get down to the business of getting the shoot organised? This is going to be the biggest for years and we will have a lot more guns. My friends are good shots and they are raring to go."

"Well, I don't know," Michael said. "Have your friends been on a shoot before this? And too many guns could be dangerous."

"Are you afraid, Michael, that my friends won't fit in? You are just as bad as father was, having to keep the old traditions with his close-knit upper-class friends."

Michael left it at that. He wasn't in the mood for arguing with him. He was so happy with the news that he was going to be a father.

CHAPTER 5

THE house, the whole estate, was a hive of activity.

Every year the shoot took in a good deal of money. The Howard estate was popular with all. It was a prestige event to shoot there. The ladies accompanied their husbands. Some of the young unattached girls would be there, hoping to find a rich husband. A picnic was held near the shoot. A large tent would be used with tables filled with mountains of food and drink. The servants would be there to serve them.

At night a meal would be served in the large dining room, the ladies in their evening gowns and the men in full evening dress.

The day of the shoot dawned—a perfect day, clear and bright with just a touch of frost, the trees glorious in all the reds and yellows of Autumn.

Kathryn got caught up in all the excitement, changed her mind about staying at the house and decided she would go with the ladies to the picnic tent. Michael looked a bit worried about this.

"Are you sure you will be okay, Kathryn?"

"Of course I will! Now off you go and enjoy yourself."

Kathryn's mother and father had arrived the night before. They were so thrilled to be grandparents. The four of them sat up well into the night.

Kathryn's mother was sad that she and her father would be away in Italy at the time of the birth and they would be gone for nearly a year. She turned to Kathryn.

"You do understand, my darling, your father can't put it off. There is so much to be sorted out over there. He is going to sell the mines to an Italian company. Your father hasn't been keeping too well recently. I feel that I have to be with him. Anyway, we have been thinking of retiring to our villa there."

"Mother, of course I understand, and one day I would love to take Michael there."

She turned to Michael.

"You would just love it. The villa is sitting near the sea in Sorrento. I have such happy memories of holidays there." She turned to her father. "Do you remember dancing the tarantella with me?"

"As if I could ever forget," he laughed. "Your wife was a wee madam," he said, turning to Michael. "We were out for the evening. Kathryn had three of her school friends visiting that Summer. Before I knew what was happening there I was, making a fool of myself dancing the tarantella. Never mind, we got a round of applause."

"Do you remember, mother, you asking the waiter where the nearest market was and he kept saying PIONA? We were in fits of laughter!"

To this day her mother said "I don't know if it was the name of the market or the name of the village."

Kathryn remembered. "I got the best shoes there that I had in my life. The old shoemaker measured my feet. I explained what I would like. He listened to me, his head to one side, then said come back maybe four hours and they will be ready. And indeed they were! Do you remember them mother? Beautiful soft brown leather polished to the colour of conkers."

Her father looked at Kathryn, her face glowing at the happy memories.

"Well then," he said, "why don't you and Michael come for a month? I'm sure Ralph could look after things here. After all, the busiest time on the farm and estate has gone."

"Oh father, oh Michael, *could* we? Could we?"

Michael hugged her. "I don't see why not. After all, we never did have a honeymoon."

And so it was decided but on the understanding that they would be home for the baby's birth.

She told the ladies all about it as they walked towards the tent.

"We had such a lovely night. Michael gets on so well with both my parents."

As they walked along one of the ladies turned round. "Who is that young boy? He always seems to be around you."

Kathryn turned. "Oh," she said. "That's Joe. He works about the yard. His father was killed here. He fell while repairing the stable roof. When he died Michael's father allowed his young son to work here. That way his mother and young brother and sister were allowed to stay on in the estate cottage. I had noticed that when I'm about he isn't far off. He is just like a little puppy. He is only about thirteen but he is a good little worker."

She turned to talk to him. "What are you carrying there, Joe?"

She looked. It was a pile of beautiful white tablecloths.

"Cook told me to take them to the picnic," he said. "They be for the tables."

Cook, too, had a soft spot for Joe. He would arrive at cockcrow every morning and she would have him in the kitchen giving him something to eat and a hot cup of tea.

One morning he was sitting as usual in the corner beside the range when Ralph came in unexpectedly. He had been out all night. He shouted at Joe and caught him at the back of the neck ready to throw him out.

Cook turned on him. "You get out! This is my kitchen. It's not time for the lad to start work".

Ralph growled but turned and left.

CHAPTER 6

RALPH remembered the times when cook had smacked him when he was a boy. Seth and cook were popular in the village. It wouldn't pay to quarrel with them.

"Do you get on with Ralph?" one of the women asked.

Kathryn thought for a moment.

"I am so very, very happy here, it doesn't really matter whether I get on with Ralph."

"A very diplomatic answer!" the women laughed.

When they arrived at the picnic everything was set out. A festive atmosphere was in the air.

Kathryn refused a glass of Champagne. "I don't need it. I'm happy to see everyone around me happy."

Apart from the waiters, all the men had gone, getting ready to take up their gun positions.

In a few minutes a whistle blew and there was a flutter of birds taking to the air. Then there was the banging of the guns. The shoot had started.

The ladies had nothing to do but sit enjoying all the news about the district.

"So you are off to Italy?" one of the ladies said to Kathryn. "You lucky thing. I was in Rome a couple of years ago. Some of the shopping there is out of this world."

"I threw money into the Trevi fountain. It's supposed to mean that I'll go back there. I hope it's true."

When the whistle went loud and shrill the ladies looked at each other. "That's strange, they have only been shooting about an hour."

A man, white faced come running up. He shouted to one of the servants: "Quick, go and fetch a doctor! There has been an accident."

There was total confusion, everyone running about. Someone pulled off the white tablecloth, scattering all the food. "We might need this," he said.

Kathryn's father, staggering like a drunk man, came up to Kathryn. He held her close. "It's Michael, he's been shot."

Kathryn started running.

"Wait, Kathryn, wait!" her father shouted, trying to keep up with her.

She kept on, heading to where a group of men were standing.

They were all silent. They moved back to let Kathryn in.

Michael was lying on the ground, a red stain on his chest. He opened his eyes.

"Oh Kathryn," he whispered. "Are you all right? Ralph said that you…" He smiled at her, and then he was gone. The red leaves of the rowan floated down and lay on his chest, their colour matching the red stain on his clothing.

Some of the men were weeping.

Kathryn bent down and kissed him, then turned to her father. "I will go back to the house now."

Nobody knew what to do or say. Then someone covered him with the white tablecloth and placed him on a cart and took him home.

Kathryn locked herself in her room. She would see no one. Her mother and father pleaded with her to come out. "Pease, Kathryn, you must eat. Remember the baby."

When she did come out after nearly a week she was just like a shadow. She attended the inquiry into Michael's death. The verdict was accidental death. Nobody knew who had fired the fatal shot.

CHAPTER 7

THE day of the funeral was a just a blur to Kathryn. She looked at the altar. No Michael standing there waiting for her to walk up the aisle, like on their wedding day.

It was his coffin that was there today. She remembered all the happiness they had shared. But over and over in her mind his last words, "Oh Kathryn, it's you. Are you all right? Ralph said that you…" He had never finished. His eyes had closed and he was gone.

What had Ralph said to him to make him run towards the tea tent? Was he running to see her? His words would stay with her forever.

A few days after Michael's funeral the owner of the village inn was taking out some empty crates to the back door.

Ralph and one of his rough friends were having an argument.

He heard Ralph say, "You will get no more money from me! You will be on the next coach to London and if I ever hear that you have opened your big mouth it will be the end of you."

The owner slipped back quietly into the inn.

♣

"Kathryn, we really have to go home. There is so much to do before we go to Italy. Why don't you come with us as we planned before?"

"Mother, the plans we had included Michael. I could never go there now."

Her mother hugged her. "Well, will you do something for me? Get in touch with Gran-Mere. She will help you and maybe the two of you could go now and again to the house just to see that everything is all right there. We have kept on the cook and one or two workers."

"Oh mother, of course I will. You know how much I love Gran-Mere."

Kathryn sat remembering Gran-Mere. Apparently when she was about three years old she had taken ill with a very high temperature. The doctor was called. He tried everything to bring the temperature down but in vain.

Then her mother told her this woman appeared. The woman had asked to see the child that was ill, saying, "I heard about it in the village."

"It was strange," her mother said. "I never questioned her but she went at once to see you. She put her hand on your forehead, felt your tummy and then said, 'I will go to the kitchen now. I will make medicine for her.' She appeared with some revolting looking liquid and fed it to you a drop at a time. She sat with you, not moving for hours. Then suddenly you were violently sick. She placed a cloth on your forehead, dipped in something sweet smelling. By evening you were sitting up in bed. We knew and the doctor knew that you had been near death and that Gran-Mere had saved your life. Nobody knew where she had come from. She had suddenly appeared in Redburn village in a cottage that had stood empty for years. Redburn village, as you know, is about seven miles from here. She must have walked all the way. She was to be seen in the forest near her cottage collecting all sorts of herbs. She spoke very little to the village people but would always help where it was needed. You always adored her, Kathryn, and she had a great fondness for you."

Kathryn missed her mother and father when they left for Italy.

She thought her father did not look well but she put it down to Michael's death.

It was weeks before she left the house after Michael's death

One day she called Joe. "I want you to get the pony and trap ready and I want you to take me to the church."

She wrapped up warmly. It was bitterly cold and snow was threatening. She slipped out of the house. The pony and trap were there but no sign of Joe.

Just then Ralph appeared. "I'm going to take you. Joe has work to do in the bottom field."

Kathryn felt uncomfortable with him but didn't want to make a fuss.

When they arrived at the church he said, "How long are you going to be? I'll come back for you."

Kathryn felt like saying, 'Where are you going that you can't wait?' but instead she said, "Not more than an hour, it will be cold in the church."

She sat in one of the pews and let the tears flow. After an age the baby stirring in her womb roused her. She was shivering with cold and the church was beginning to get dark inside.

She hurried outside, expecting Ralph to be waiting but there was no sign of him. She was cold and angry. She started to walk. Surely he couldn't be far off.

She walked and walked. The darkness was coming down. Her legs felt weak. The snow that had been threatening all day started in earnest and with the north wind blowing into her face, she could hardly breathe. She felt so weak that all she wanted to do was lie down.

She heard the sound of the pony and trap. Thank God at last Ralph had returned for her. Bit it wasn't Ralph, it was Joe. He helped her up and wrapped a blanket round her.

When they arrived back at the house Joe shouted for cook. She helped her up to bed but her shivering couldn't stop. The doctor was called.

"You had a lucky escape, my girl. You could have died out there if Joe hadn't come in time."

She was nearly a week in bed. When she challenged Ralph and asked him why he had not returned to the church for her he just shrugged his shoulders. "I had business in Trent. I didn't know that I had to take you home."

She wanted to shout at him, 'Liar, liar! You wanted me to die out there!'—but she said nothing.

She had a feeling of dread for herself and her baby. 'We are standing in his way owning the estate,' she thought. Why had she not realised it sooner?

When she spoke to Joe he was nearly in tears. "I was ready to take you but Ralph sent me away to the bottom field. There was nothing urgent to do there. I came back when it started to get dark. I asked cook if you were home. The pony and trap were back in the stable. Cook said that Ralph had brought it back and then had gone riding away. Cook thought you were about the house somewhere but there was no sign of you. That was when I decided to look for you."

CHAPTER 8

A FEW days later Kathryn was sitting in the lounge wondering how she could bear to live in this house, always wondering what Ralph was up to.

She heard shouting and screaming coming from the yard. She rushed out.

Ralph was lashing out with his whip at someone lying on the ground. "I'll teach you, you thieving brat!" he was roaring.

Kathryn rushed over. To her horror she saw that it was Joe lying there trying to cover his face from the cruel whip. She rushed at Ralph. "You beast, leave him alone!" One of the stable men grabbed hold of the whip and it looked for a moment that he would use it on Ralph.

Kathryn helped Joe up. Lying on the ground beside him were some potatoes and vegetables. "I never stole them," Joe was sobbing. "The old master and master Michael let me have them to help us out at home."

Kathryn helped him into the house. She bathed and bandaged his legs that were badly cut with the whip.

Joe struggled up. "My mother will be worried. I'll have to go home. What's going to happen if Ralph won't let me work here anymore?"

"Don't worry about that, Joe. Tell me, why has Ralph been so bad to you recently?"

Joe hung his head. "I can't tell you."

"Come, Joe. I'll take you home and on the way I insist that you tell me. You saved my life, Joe. I must find out what's going on."

"I'm afraid of Ralph," he began. "If I talk he will harm me and the family and we will be thrown out of the cottage. I always tried to stay near you to be safe from him."

"What happened, Joe? Don't be afraid to tell me." As Joe started to talk Kathryn's blood went cold.

"I was down at the river weeks ago. I was looking for duck eggs. I was crawling among the reeds. I wouldn't have taken all the eggs, just one from each nest. An old man came along. He looked a bit like a tramp. I kept hidden. He was looking around as if expecting someone there. I heard a horse. I looked up from behind the reeds. It was Ralph. He jumped off the horse and went towards the old man. They stood talking for a minute, and then they started to argue. Ralph pushed him. The old man fell and then..." Joe stopped, his whole body shaking.

Kathryn put her arm round him "Carry on Joe, you must tell me."

"The old man was lying on the ground. He was shouting 'I'm your father, I'm your father!' Ralph lifted a stone and struck him on the head. Then he pulled him into the deep part of the river.

"I started to run but Ralph looked up and saw me. I know that one day he will kill me to keep me quiet. I never told my mother. Please don't tell her," he pleaded.

"I'm coming to talk to your mother. Don't worry, I will just tell her about Ralph whipping you."

As Joe talked Kathryn realised that Joe would never be safe working on the estate. But a plan was forming in her mind.

Joe's mother was at the door waiting for him. She was surprised to see Kathryn. His young brother and sister were hiding behind her. She invited Kathryn in; then she noticed that Joe was limping. "Oh Joe! What has happened? Have you had an accident?"

"I will explain," Kathryn said, and she told her what had happened. "Ralph is not a good person and Joe will not be safe from his anger. He won't be able to work there anymore."

"Oh God, what will we do? How will we manage?"

The little boy came from behind his mother. "Don't worry mum, I'll help."

His mother hugged and kissed him. "Oh Peter, I'm sure you will."

Kathryn smiled. She looked round the room. It had only a few bits of furniture but everything was clean and shining.

She turned to Joe's mother. "I'm sorry we haven't been introduced. We only spoke of you as Joe's mother."

"I'm Jessie Brown, madam, and these are my children, Peter and Sally."

"Now, Mrs Brown, I have, I think, a solution. You may have heard that my mother and father have gone to Italy."

Jessie Brown nodded.

"Well, they have left their house with only a cook and a couple of their workers. Now it's a big house and for the year they are away, half of it has been closed up. How would you all like to go and live there? You wouldn't have to pay rent and there would be plenty work for Joe and you too could work in the house. Of course, you would be paid."

Joe and his mother looked at each other.

"It would be like heaven," his mother said.

"Now that is settled, let me warn you, Ralph must know nothing about it. I will travel with you. You must pack only your clothes and a few precious bits. I will get one of the men I trust to drive the coach. I will make arrangements when I go home and you will be ready tomorrow morning."

She turned to Joe. "Don't worry, everything will be all right."

So it was that early the next morning the coach arrived at the little cottage. It stopped close to the door so that nobody could spot the little family going into it and nobody thought anything of Kathryn going to check her parents' house.

Kathryn stayed overnight at her old home to get the family settled in.

Before she left the next morning she gave a letter to Mrs. Brown stating that it could be their home as long as they wished to stay there. She wished that she could have stayed there but she made up her mind that her visits there would be frequent.

Weeks passed. She saw very little of Ralph. He said very little of the disappearance of Joe's family and only a short time after they had gone he moved two of his rough friends into the cottage.

Kathryn was nearly seven months pregnant. Only another two months to go. She felt restless. She couldn't settle to anything. She decided to visit her old home for a few weeks. She got in touch with Gran-Mere. She had promised her mother she would.

CHAPTER 9

RALPH was making her feel more and more uncomfortable. He had moved more and more of his friends into the house, replacing the loyal staff that had worked there for years. The only one left was cook. She knew she should have stood up to him but after Michael's death the heart had gone out of her.

She managed to see Katy who kept telling her to stand up to him.

Kathryn felt great relief when she was back in her old home. Gran-Mere was there to meet her.

"You look quite ill, my child. I'm glad I'm here to look after you."

Kathryn told Gran-Mere about Ralph and her worries that he would harm her and, more especially, the baby who would be the heir to the estate.

It was during the night that the first pains started. Kathryn shouted for Gran-Mere. All night and into the next day the pains never stopped. The doctor couldn't get through to the house. The snow had caused a landslide.

The baby arrived just as the dawn was breaking. Gran-Mere held it up to Kathryn, a beautiful little girl. Just then the doctor arrived. He looked at Gran-Mere and shook his head.

Kathryn whispered to Gran-Mere, "Don't let Ralph know about the baby." She held the doctor's hand. She made him swear to secrecy. When she told him the reason he agreed.

"There is no need to tell him," he said. "He isn't a relative, but your mother and father must be told."

Kathryn's voice grew weaker. "Gran-Mere," she whispered. "promise me you will take my baby and look after her."

"I promise you," Gran-Mere said, but she and the doctor were unable to stop her haemorrhaging. She opened her eyes and smiled at them—and then she was gone.

Gran-Mere wrapped the baby warmly and carried her under her cloak and slipped quietly out the back door.

Kathryn was laid to rest beside Michael.

CHAPTER 10

"TANSY, where are you, child?" Gran-Mere was shouting from the cottage door. "Come along. We must go to the village at once. A little baby is very ill."

A little girl appeared. She was carrying a bunch of bluebells. "Look Gran-Mere, I picked them for you."

Gran-mere looked at her, long hair the colour of ripened corn, and eyes that matched the colour of the bluebells she was carrying.

Gran-Mere felt a tug at her heart. It was four years since she had carried her, a new born baby under her cloak, promising her dying mother that she would keep her safe. She remembered the long walk, falling into snowdrifts, thinking she would never make it home.

"Gran-Mere," the child was tugging at her skirt. "I thought we had to go to the village?"

"Yes we do. Wait a moment. I must get my basket."

The child knew that Gran-Mere never went anywhere without her basket. It was always full of all sorts of herbs.

"The magic basket," the child called it, because it made sick people better.

They hurried down the road, the tall foreign looking woman dressed completely in black and the little girl almost running to keep up with her.

When they arrived at the cottage a group of women were at the door.

"You are too late," one woman sobbed. "The baby has just died."

Gran-Mere ignored her and carried on inside.

Doctor Brown was consoling the mother.

"How long has the baby gone?" she demanded of the doctor.

"Just a minute ago," he said.

Gran-Mere lifted the baby, a little boy. She placed him on the floor and loosened his clothing. The mother shouted at her and tried to pull Gran-Mere away from the baby. The doctor held her back.

Then Gran-Mere knelt down and started to breathe into the baby's mouth. At the same time she seemed to massage its chest.

She kept doing this for what seemed ages.

The doctor said, "I think you will have to give up, Gran-Mere. You can't save this one."

"What do you mean?" the mother was shouting at the doctor.

"I have seen her do this before," the doctor said. "And the child lived."

Just then to all those in the room a miracle happened. The baby started to cry—a whimper at first; then it gave a loud cry. The women at the door heard it. Some of the women crossed themselves. How could the doctor say the baby was dead and now it was alive?

The doctor and Gran-Mere smiled at each other. The doctor had already seen some of Gran-Mere's amazing work.

Gran-Mere turned to the child sitting quietly in the corner while it was all going on. "Come now, Tansy," she said. "Let's go home."

The next day as they were walking to the store in the village, young boys sitting on a wall shouted at them: "Witch, witch, where's your broomstick?" And Gran-Mere knew that some of the village really did think she was a witch, and she knew that it was going to be difficult shielding Tansy from some ignorant people.

Gran-Mere was always with Tansy when they walked to the village and even though the cottage was near the village, they kept to themselves and the villagers only called at the cottage to ask Gran-Mere for help when there was illness.

Tansy never missed the company of other children. Her days were happy and full. In the Summer and Spring she roamed the forest with Gran-Mere, collecting herbs. She loved the forest. On warm days she would paddle in the stream, then sit in the shade in their favourite little dell among the primroses and wild violets. Gran-Mere would explain all the uses of the herbs.

They were sitting there one lovely summer's morning when they heard a great deal of shouting and thrashing about in the forest.

A young fox in its panic ran straight into where they were sitting. Gran-Mere, quick as a flash, threw the blanket they had been sitting on over the fox, covering it up completely.

The fox lay still, too exhausted to move. Gran-Mere threw some sweet smelling herbs over the blanket and some on the grass a little away from them. "That should throw them off the scent," she said.

The dogs appeared first. They halted near them, sniffing and scraping the ground, then off they went. Gran-Mere sighed with relief.

Then the men appeared on their horses. One of them who appeared to be the leader halted near them. He spoke to Gran-Mere.

"Have you seen the fox? It was heading this way."

Gran-Mere shook her head.

A young boy who was with them, not much older than Tansy, smiled at her and looked towards the blanket.

"Come father," he said. "We will lose the dogs." And off they galloped.

Gran-Mere removed the blanket. The fox lay quite still for a moment. It looked at them before racing off into the forest.

"Well well," Gran-Mere said. "That was Sir Edward Frail and the young lad, his son, Ian. They live in that big house you can see from the cottage. The forest and the village belong to him. The Frails made their money with grocery stores all over the country." With mischief in her eyes, Gran-Mere added: "You could call them grocers."

"The boy was nice," Tansy said. "He knew the fox was hidden under the blanket."

The years were passing quickly, happy contented years. Gran-Mere and Tansy still kept apart from the village people.

Tansy was quick and bright at all the lessons that Gran-Mere gave her. Her French was as fluent as Gran-Mere's and often they carried out conversations in it. And of course when they were overheard it convinced the villagers of how strange they were.

Tansy, nearly ten years old now, started to get a mind of her own. She wished she could play with the village children.

One day Gran-Mere took ill. She was unable to go to the village.

"Could you go, Tansy? I promised the butcher's wife some rosemary. She is suffering from bad headaches and if she puts it in her pillow it will ease the pain."

Tansy set off to the village. She felt a mixture of fear and excitement. It was her first visit to the village on her own. She walked quickly past the spot where the village children gathered. She breathed a sigh of relief. There was no sign of them today. She quickly delivered the rosemary, then started to hurry home.

CHAPTER 11

TANSY was just passing the usual spot where the children gathered, and there they were, boys and girls. There seemed to be dozens of them.

One of the girls shouted, "Come on boys, here comes the witch's girl!"

They surrounded her. Tansy, terrified, tried to get away.

One of the girls pulled her hair. "Look, it's fair. Does it turn black at night when you ride your broomstick?"

A boy with the brightest red hair that Tansy had ever seen and a face covered in freckles pushed his way in and stood beside Tansy.

"Leave her alone!" he shouted at them.

He turned to the girl that had pulled her hair.

"You're just jealous, Jessie Campbell, because she is much prettier than you."

The children backed away. The boy with the red hair seemed to be the leader.

He turned to Tansy, his face blushing scarlet. "Why don't you come to play with us? We have lots of fun."

"I don't think Gran-Mere will allow me," she said. But at the same time she thought, 'I'm going to do it! I will come down here to play with them.'

Redburn village was one of the many small villages spreading like a string of pearls, all leading eventually to London. Each small village was self-contained with its own customs. Some of the locals had never moved from their own village, quite content to spend their whole lives there, caring nothing for what went on in the outside world.

The church and some of the houses outside the village belonging to the doctor and some of the shop owners were strong solid buildings. Along the main village street where nearly all the villagers lived was a different story. The rows of thatched cottages, no better than hovels, looked as if the inhabitants had given up the struggle to keep them repaired and clean. Some of the broken windows had been replaced by boards. It did look as if one or two of the inhabitants had tried to make a garden round the house but had given up. They were covered now with rubbish and nettles.

Along the front of the cottages a stream no better than a drain was used to throw all their slops. In the Winter months when there was plenty of rain it wasn't so bad, but in the good weather the stench was unbearable.

Sir Edward had stopped charging rent in the cottages years before, leaving it to the inhabitants to do their own repairs, but because there was no one in authority to tell them what to do, everything was left to go to ruin.

Redburn village was different from Trent village. In Trent the majority worked in the Howard estate. It gave the village some security.

Tansy managed to persuade Gran-Mere to let her play with the village children and she loved running down to the village to play with them. Her great friend Tom Bruce, the red-headed boy, she followed everywhere. He was her hero.

One day when they were playing hopscotch in the square he said to Tansy, "I have to go home to get money for the bakers. I promised my mother. She is a bit poorly and can't go herself. You stay here with the others. I won't be long."

Tansy got bored with the game and went off to meet him. He lived in one of the cottages. She shouted for him and when there was no reply she knocked at the half open door and went in. She was horrified. The room seemed so dark. A poor fire was belching out clouds of smoke. There was a bed in the corner. A man was lying on it. A bandage round his chest was oozing blood.

Tansy thought he was dead. She screamed. A woman came out of a bedroom. She stood swaying at the bedroom door. Tansy thought she was going to fall but she managed to make her way to a chair.

She was just a small women and Tansy, even as a child, thought she must have been pretty with her red hair. She knew it was Tom's mother but she also knew, with all the visits she had been on visiting the sick with Gran-Mere, that she was very ill.

Tom appeared. He was carrying a loaf of bread. He was angry, seeing Tansy in the house. "I told you to wait. You shouldn't have come in here."

"I'm sorry, Tom. Your mother looks ill. I'm sure I could help. I could go and fetch Gran-Mere."

"I will be fine, my dear," she whispered. "Don't worry about me."

Tom turned to Tansy. "Mum has been ill for nearly a week. A lot of people in the village have been ill."

"Why did you not send for a doctor or even Gran-Mere?" Tansy demanded.

"We couldn't let anyone in the house," Tom's mother answered.

Tom finished talking for her. "Dad was poaching and he was shot by one of the bailiffs. He managed to get away but if they find out it was him he could go to prison. He did earn a little money doing odd jobs about the village but when they stopped there was no money coming in. He had to poach."

CHAPTER 12

WHEN Tansy went home and told Gran-Mere the story, she immediately put on her cloak and filled her basket with herbs. Another basket she handed to Tansy with strips of fresh white linen and jars of ointments. They set out for the Bruces' cottage.

Gran-Mere took charge as soon as she entered the cottage.

"Go and fetch some firewood," she said to Tom. And to Tansy, "Fill the kettle, I want boiling water. I will attend to your Dad first."

Tom's father was almost unconscious. Gran-Mere removed the bandage and flung it on the fire. With a piece of clean linen rung out in the boiled water she commenced to clean the wound. He groaned in pain.

Gran-Mere kept talking as she worked. "The bullet has not done much damage. It's the dirt that has gone into the wound that has caused the most damage."

She mixed herbs in boiling water and made a paste. She placed it on the wound, then bandaged it up with more clean linen. "I will come in tomorrow and change the dressing." She turned to Tom's mother who had sat quietly, too weak to speak. "Now Mrs Bruce," Gran-Mere said, "have you vomited?" When the woman nodded, Gran-Mere asked, "Have you had diarrhoea?" Again Mrs Bruce nodded. "Have you been near the burn?"

The woman whispered, "I went into it with some of the neighbours to rescue a cow that had got stuck there."

"That filthy burn," Gran-Mere muttered to herself. "Something will have to be done about it."

She made a drink with more herbs and stood over Tom's mother till she had drunk it all. She turned to Tom. "I am making another jug full. You will give it to both your mother and father in a few hours. Take your mother to bed. Have you got warming stones?" He nodded. "Put them in the bed. Your mother must be kept warm."

In a few days both Tom's mother and father were up.

A strange thing happened a few days later. A group of men from Sir Edward's estate appeared and for days they worked digging out the burn and making it deeper so that the water flowed quickly, getting rid of the waste and a lot of germs lying in it.

Was it because the women had saved the cow belonging to Sir Edward, or because someone had the courage to go and complain about the burn to Sir Edward?

Stranger still, one of Sir Edward's managers came to offer Tom's father a job keeping the paths clear in the forest—work that could be his for life.

"Gran-Mere," Tansy said, "tonight is Hallowe'en. Can I go out with Tom and the rest of the children? They call it guising. They dress up and wear masks and go round the houses and pretend they are ghosts."

"Child, child, do stop prattling on. Of course I know about Hallowe'en and yes, you can go. We will need to think of something for you to wear."

So Tansy, all excited, dressed up with bits and pieces to look like an old woman, her hair hidden under one of Gran-Mere's shawls, and set off to the village.

Tansy had never known such fun. They went from house to house, sometimes singing or reciting a poem and into the bag they were carrying given sweets and nuts.

Tom, as usual, was the leader, and it was at his suggestion that they visit Sir Edward's orchard and scrump for apples. "It's not really stealing," he said to Tansy and the other children. "They will be lying on the ground and they would just go rotten."

One or two of the children didn't want to go and one by one they ran off.

Tansy and Tom and just another two or three were left. "Let's go," said Tom. "I know where to get over the wall."

Tansy found it difficult trying to jump into the garden with the long dress she was wearing. Tom shouted: "Look, there are some sacks beside the wall. Jump onto them."

Tansy landed on them with a bump. They started to gather the apples. The ground was covered with them.

Tom had just whispered, "We mustn't make any noise," when suddenly a bright light shone on them. "So what have we here?" A man's voice shouted. The children, blinded by the light, at first saw two men.

Tom grabbed Tansy's hand. "Come on, run for it!" The men chased them. The other children managed to climb the wall and get away but, as before, Tansy's dress held her back. She couldn't get over the wall.

One of the men caught hold of her and the other man grabbed Tom who was struggling to get away.

"Right," the man said. "Up to the house with you, pals. We will see what Sir Edward has to say about young thieves."

So they were led into the house. There seemed to be a party going on. There was a lot of children as well as grown ups. They all stared at the children.

A man that Tansy recognised as Sir Edward came towards them. "So we have two guisers," he said

One of the men said, "They were stealing the apples. It's two of the village brats."

One of the children came over to them. A young girl was wearing the loveliest dress Tansy had ever seen. It was pale blue and pink. The girl, though pretty, had a scowl on her face. She stood right in front of

Tansy and then started to laugh.

"Well well," she said, "if it isn't the nasty little witch's girl." Then Tansy remembered. This was the girl that Gran-Mere had scolded when she had seen her throwing stones at a young dog.

She pulled the shawl from Tansy's head. "We could duck her in the tub?"

"Yes, let's!" the children shouted.

Tansy looked in the middle of the room. There was a large tub of water that had been used for ducking apples.

"Leave her alone!" Tom shouted at the girls.

Just then a young boy came into the room. "What's going on? What's all the noise?"

Tansy looked at him. It was Ian, Sir Edward's son.

Sir Edward was smiling. "Well Ian, what shall we do with them? They have been stealing apples from the orchard."

"I think she should be ducked," the girl said again.

Ian turned to her. "Would *you* like to be ducked?" She was furious and stalked away.

"Well," Sir Edward said. "Since it is Hallowe'en, I think that you two should sing or recite."

"I can't sing," said Tom.

"I can," Tansy said. "I will sing a French song that Gran-Mere taught me."

She started to sing. The whole room went quiet. Her voice rose sweet but strong, rising to the roof. When she finished there was silence; then they all stood to clap.

Ian took her hand. "You can have as much sweets and apples that you can carry, both of you." He turned to his father. "That would be fair, Dad, wouldn't it?"

"Much more than fair, my Son. I have never heard such a beautiful voice." He turned to Tansy. "Thank you, my dear. We will take you both home safely. I for one will never forget this Hallowe'en."

CHAPTER 13

THE day before Tansy's sixteenth birthday, Dr Brown went to visit Gran-Mere. Tansy was out visiting one of Dr Brown's patients. For the past few years she had been helping him. Dr Brown was growing to rely on her more and more.

He looked at Gran-Mere. She had aged a lot in the last few years and Dr Brown suspected that she was in lot of pain but wouldn't admit it.

They had been close friends since the night of Tansy's birth and it was Dr Brown who gave Gran-Mere the news of what was happening in Trent.

Kathryn on her deathbed had signed all the documents making sure of Tansy's inheritance. They were put into Dr Brown's hands for safekeeping.

Kathryn's parents had not managed to attend her funeral as four months after their arrival in Italy her father had a stroke and her mother couldn't leave him.

Everything in Italy had been a big disappointment to them. The people they were doing business with were not entirely honest and the long shot was that they lost a great deal of money. Eventually their house and home that Kathryn had lived in had to be sold.

The new owners, though they were kind enough, did not like the idea of Joe and his family living there, but gave them the choice of living at the gatehouse. They were quite happy to go there. Joe's brother and sister were both married and now lived in London.

Kathryn's mother and father had both died within a year of each other. They never got over Kathryn's death.

Dr Brown heard a lot of stories coming out of Trent.

Ralph had continued drinking and gambling over the years. The estate was suffering and only a few of the old workers were left and they were the ones who kept things going. Of course all the workers that he had brought in to replace the old workers were friends of his who drank and gambled with him.

Dr Brown said: "What are we to do, Gran-Mere?"

"We must tell Tansy that the estate is hers. If we don't, there will be no estate left. She has already lost her grandparents' house and money."

Gran-Mere nodded. "I knew that the time must come and in ordinary circumstances I would have told her years ago, but I was always frightened that she would tell the wrong people and that Ralph would find out who she was. But Doctor, let me find the right time. For her sixteenth birthday I want to take her to London to buy clothes and she has never stopped talking about a dance to be held in the village hall next week and she must have a new dress."

So it was decided and the next day they set off. The coach journey seemed endless to Tansy. She had been to London before with Gran-Mere but this time it was different. She felt so grown up. And Gran-Mere had said she could choose her own dress!

The coach dropped them off in Trafalgar Square. They were immediately surrounded by pigeons.

"Some people hate them but I think they give visitors a welcome to London," Gran-Mere said. After a pause, she continued, "Now, first of all I have to visit the solicitors. I have some business to discuss with them."

They went to a very impressive building near the square. 'Young and Dobie Solicitors,' it stated on a glass door.

"You wait here in the hall, I won't be long." True to her word she was out in no time.

"Let's go now," she said. "I think we should go for a meal. It's going to be a long day."

Everything seemed wonderful to Tansy—the restaurant they ate in, the tables with their snow white tablecloths, all the silver and flowers everywhere.

"Oh Gran-Mere, this must be expensive."

"It is," she replied. "But it is your special day."

They started off shopping—not in little shops down side streets, but in beautiful expensive shops where a man in uniform opened the doors for them.

Beautifully dressed women showed them to gilt chairs where they sat as mannequins paraded, showing off the clothes. Gran-Mere would look at everything and if she wasn't satisfied she just waved her hand. More and more clothes were shown. She would turn to Tansy. "Do you like this or that?"

Soon Tansy had capes, skirts, hats, muffs—box after box to be delivered on the first coach to Redburn.

"Now, Tansy, about this dress. I know exactly the shop we must go to."

She spoke to the doorman. A coach pulled up to the door. The doorman helped them into the coach and it took them straight to the shop for the dress. Again they were ushered in and as dress after dress was paraded in front of them, Tansy just looked at them until one particular dress was brought out.

Tansy jumped to her feet.

"Oh Gran-Mere, please *please*, this is the one! I just love it."

Gran-Mere smiled. "You, my darling," she said, "you have good taste. It is a beautiful dress." Yards and yards of white velvet flowed from a vee-shaped waist. The sweet heart neckline was edged with the finest lace and to match there was a tiny lace bolero.

CHAPTER 14

THE dress was a perfect fit. No alteration was needed!

"Now," said Gran-Mere, "we will visit another department for underwear."

Tansy's excitement was catching. The assistants couldn't do enough for her.

Gran-Mere started to look tired. "Oh, I'm so sorry, Gran-Mere. Let's go and maybe have tea."

They sat in a little teashop, which was quiet and peaceful, and soon Gran-Mere was her old self.

"Now Tansy, before we go home, I want you to see another part of London."

They left the big stores and clean streets and Gran-Mere said, "Hold my hand, Tansy, and hold tight to your bag."

Tansy was horrified. The streets were full of rubbish. The houses leading on to the street seemed to have women in every door shouting and yelling at each other. And when Gran-Mere and Tansy passed, out they came on to the street shouting abuse at them. Some of the children dressed in rags, pulled at their skirts. "Give us a penny, Missus," they called, snots hanging from their noses.

At a butcher's shop the meat hanging outside was covered in flies.

The stench in the whole street was sickening.

Tansy, almost in tears, pleaded: "Please let's get away from here."

They turned and left. "You had to see it," Gran-Mere said. "The poor in London are some of the poorest in the country."

"But surely, Gran-Mere, they are all so dirty. Surely they can wash?"

"Did you notice in that whole street there was only one water pump? And sometimes they don't work properly. A cake of soap is quite a luxury. Close by there is a soap factory but the workers are paid so poorly that they can't afford to buy it." She continued, kindly, "Come now, my dear. You have seen both sides of London. Let's go home now."

Tansy was thinking constantly about the dance.

It was Sir Edward that was organising it. It always took place in the village hall because even though Sir Edward's home had a large ballroom it wasn't big enough for over three hundred people who were invited. Sir Edward had the dance every year in celebration of Ian's birth.

The musicians were coming from London. As well as the flowers to decorate the hall, all sorts of fancy goods would also be coming from London.

The village trades people were not left out. All the meats and vegetables were from the village.

Tansy and Gran-Mere were up late one night sorting out all the new clothes bought in London.

There was a knock at the door. Tansy and Gran-Mere looked at each other.

"You better answer it, Tansy. I can't, I'm in my night clothes."

Tansy, a bit scared, drew the bolts in the door. A little boy was standing there. "Can you come quickly, Miss? It's my mum. She is ill. She told me to fetch you."

"Of course, I'll come. You come inside. I won't be a minute."

"No no," the child said. "I must run home to mum. You know the house. You came there when I was ill."

Tansy looked at him closely. Of course she remembered. He had been badly scalded on his legs when a kettle had fallen off the fire. He had been such a brave little boy when she and Gran-Mere had applied all the healing herbs.

Tansy went in to get her cloak and Gran-Mere's basket.

Gran-Mere was worried. "I don't like the idea of you going out alone. There is no moon tonight and it's pitch black out there. And have you forgotten about the Black Coach?" The stories about a black coach and black horses thundering through the village, usually late at night, had been the talk of the village for weeks. The villagers were terrified. In their minds it was something evil. Nobody knew where it came from or where it went.

Neither Gran-Mere nor Tansy had seen or heard it because their cottage was a distance from the village street.

"You go to bed, Gran-Mere, and leave the light on for me."

Tansy set off. As soon as she entered the child's house she saw what was wrong with his mother. She was going to have a baby and by the looks of her she was due to give birth at any moment.

Quickly Tansy got her into bed, hoping that there would be no complications.

"Where is Dr brown?" she asked.

"He is away out on another call."

"Thank God you are here," the woman groaned as another pain shook her.

Tansy knew that the woman's husband was working away in another village and only managed to be home every Sunday.

Tansy started to get things ready for the baby. The mother had already prepared a cot for the baby, an old drawer but covered lovingly in coloured blankets.

Another shout of pain from the mother and the baby was born, a healthy baby girl. A neighbour came bursting in. "You should have come for me but I'm glad you were here," she said to Tansy. "I'll watch over them now. Go home lass, it's getting late for you to be out"

Tansy lifted her long hair and pushed it under a snood. "It takes such a long time to dry when it gets wet," she explained. Then putting the hood of her cloak over it she ventured outside. The neighbour was right. Since she had entered the house the wind and rain had got worse but it didn't worry her too much. She didn't have far to go.

What happened next she only remembered vaguely. She had been walking carefully. She heard the sound of a coach and looked round. The next recollection was of two men bending over her and the voices of women in the background. She thought they must be in the coach. One woman was saying, "She is alive, come on, let's go." And then one of the men—the older of the two, judging from his voice, for she could see nothing—pulled the hood down from the cloak. In a dazed way the voice, coming from a great distance, shouted, "Bring that lantern closer." He held it near her; then he gave a big bellow: "Look, look at the mark on her neck, it's a star! It's the same as the one Michael had and his father before him. It's a family birthmark. I'm cursed!" he raved. "That star haunts me. Who is this wench?"

A woman shouted, "Come on Ralph, let's go." The coach moved off.

Tansy couldn't remember how long she lay there. The next thing she saw was Gran-Mere bending over her. She was crying, "My child, what happened to you?" She helped her up and the two of them staggered home.

Gran-Mere took off her wet clothes and after making sure that there were no bad injuries, she put her to bed. She gave her something to drink and it was morning before she woke. Gran-Mere was sitting by her bedside. "Can you tell me, Tansy, what happened last night? I couldn't make sense of anything you said. You kept talking about a coach. Do you think it could have been the black coach that knocked you into the ditch?"

Tansy repeated to Gran-Mere everything she could remember and when she told her about a woman telling Ralph to hurry up, Gran-Mere went pale. "Oh my God," she said. "I knew it would happen one day."

CHAPTER 15

"GRAN-MERE, what's wrong? You have gone quite pale."

Gran-Mere felt her way to a chair. "Tansy, I want you to sit down. I have a lot to tell you." When she had composed herself, she continued: "Tansy, what I have to tell you started even before you were born. I have kept quiet all these years. Many times I have been tempted to tell you but I have kept quiet out of fear for your safety, so please don't be angry with me. I have loved you more than life itself."

"Oh Gran-Mere, you *know* I love you. Nothing you will say will change that."

So Gran-Mere started to talk. She told her about her mother and father, the fears that her mother had about Ralph doing harm to her baby.

"Was I the baby, Gran-Mere?" Tansy asked.

So Gran-Mere told how she had carried her away to safety, promising her dying mother that she would always keep her safe.

So she went on. She told her all about the Howard estate, which really belonged to her, and how her father's adopted brother Ralph would even commit murder to own it.

"Your birth was kept quiet. Ralph thought that you had died at birth. Dr Brown was with us and he agreed to help. Your mother had thought about everything and Dr Brown has got all the necessary papers in safe keeping." She paused. "Remember me visiting a firm of solicitors when we were in London? Well, they are the solicitors who have kept the estate safe for you."

"Oh Gran-Mere, I can't take it all in. I own an *estate*? But Gran-Mere, I am so happy here—I don't think I want the estate. Let this Ralph have it."

"It's not so simple, my darling. I wish it were. The Howard estate has been in your family for many generations. A whole village depends on it for work." She looked serious. "I think when you had the accident Ralph recognised you. He may have seen the star mark on your neck."

"I think you are right, Gran-Mere. I can remember a man shouting something about a star."

"It's a Howard mark," Gran-Mere said. "All the Howards have this birthmark on their neck. Oh Tansy, I am so worried." She continued. telling her about some of the wicked things that Ralph had done. "I think he is possessed by the devil. And all the people he gathers round him are just as bad."

Tansy was looking more and more upset.

"What am I to do, Gran-Mere? I don't want to leave Redburn."

"Now, Tansy, first things first. We must get you fit and well for the dance. Dr Brown is going to take you there and take you home afterwards."

"But Gran-Mere, the hall is just at the end of the road. I can walk there."

"And get your beautiful dress all muddy? I think not; and besides, I don't like the sound of that wind. By tomorrow night it could be quite stormy." She paused thoughtfully. "I do miss Tom so much since he went to London. I hope he is getting on all right there. I feel that he should be here for the dance. He has turned into a fine young man—with a clever head on his shoulders. Both Dr Brown and Sir Edward noticed this. I think it was Dr Brown that first drew attention to the lad, asking Sir Edward if he could arrange something for him. I believe he wants to be a solicitor."

"Do you know, Gran-Mere, that Halloween, when we went to raid Sir Edward's orchard—it changed the lives of Tom's mother and father, and Tom's."

'And maybe yours too,' Gran-Mere thought to herself.

Gran-Mere had been right as Tansy got ready for the dance, for the wind howled round the house. They could hear the branches snapping in the forest and the house seemed to shake to its very foundations.

Tansy grew more and more impatient with Gran-Mere as she brushed her hair. It fell in a shining mass to her waist. Then Gran-Mere helped her into her dress. There was a tear in her eye as she looked at her. She reminded her of her mother, but if anything, she was even more beautiful than Kathryn had been.

They were ready when Dr Brown arrived. He looked at Tansy. He couldn't be more proud of her had she been his own daughter. He would be sad to see her leave Redburn.

They arrived at the hall. Coaches seemed to be arriving from all directions, their lanterns swinging in the wind, the shouting of the coachmen trying to beat each other to be near the door.

Tansy just loved it, with all the excitement! She gasped when they entered the hall. It no longer looked like the village hall. Mountains of flowers reached to near the top of the walls, and the musicians on the stage were surrounded by ferns.

All the colours of the beautiful dresses were dazzling.

Sir Edward and Lady Frail were standing at the door to meet all the guests.

Lady Frail spoke to Tansy. "How beautiful you look, my dear. Sir Edward told me about your lovely voice singing at the Halloween party. I was sorry to have missed that party. I was detained in London, but maybe I'll hear you another time. Here comes Ian, our son. You have already met."

Ian smiled at Tansy. He asked Dr Brown if he could have the next dance with Tansy.

"Of course, young man, you may."

Tansy looked round at the other dancers. One girl, pretty in a beautiful yellow dress, was glaring at her as she danced with Ian. Suddenly Tansy recognised her. It was the girl who wanted to duck her in the tub at Sir Edward's party years before.

CHAPTER 16

DR BROWN and Sir Edward were in deep conversation when they returned from the dance floor. Dr Brown turned to Tansy. "Sir Edward was just wondering if you would be interested in going to London for voice training and maybe even to Italy after that."

Tansy looked at Sir Edward. "How wonderful that would be! But I am afraid that it would be impossible. It seems that my future has already been laid out for me."

All the young men seemed to want to dance with Tansy. She loved every minute. She decided to go to the corner of the hall where the refreshments were being served to get a lemonade.

"Oh Tansy, isn't it wonderful!" a voice said behind her. It was Jessie Campbell.

"Oh Jessie, I am sorry. I never noticed you among all this crowd."

She had become friendly with Jessie over the years. Two young village girls growing up together.

Tansy felt someone push her. The next minute her beautiful white dress was covered down the side in red wine.

"Oh, I am so sorry," a voice said.

Tansy turned. It was the girl in the yellow dress—the girl of the Halloween party.

Jessie Campbell shouted at her. "Sorry? You are *not* sorry. I saw it—you done it deliberately!"

Tansy, nearly in tears, let Jessie take her to the ladies room. Most of the wine sponged off leaving only a pale pink stain.

"You won't notice it at the dance among all the crowd," Jessie persuaded her.

Lady Frail came into the ladies room. "My dear, how unfortunate."

"My Lady," Jessie piped up. "Unfortunately nothing, that girl done it deliberately. I think she is a friend of your ladyship."

"Are you sure?" Lady Frail said.

"That's Eva Williams. Her father is a business partner of Sir Edward."

"I'm afraid she's a bit spoilt. Maybe she didn't like you dancing with Ian. She seems to think Ian is her property. Please don't let it spoil the dance for you. Your friend is right. It's hardly noticeable."

Later in the evening Dr Brown came up to Tansy.

"Are you all right, my dear? The dance is coming to an end now. In spite of what happened to your dress, did you enjoy yourself?"

"Oh yes, Doctor. It was the best night of my whole life and I'm sure Gran-Mere will work her magic on the dress and it will be as good as new again."

Dr Brown turned to Jessie Campbell. "I was wanting to have a word with you, Jessie. I was looking for someone to look after the house for me, maybe cook a light meal. It would of course be live in. The whole place has been sadly neglected over the years since my wife died. I won't be able to pay you much but you would have a nice room and good food."

"Don't say another word, Dr Brown," Jessie said, flushing with excitement. "I would love to work for you." She turned to Tansy. "Imagine, Tansy—me living in that big house! I will be so happy there."

Dr Brown smiled. He knew that Jessie had a miserable life since her father died and her mother had remarried. Her stepfather was a bit of a waster and was not above lashing out at Jessie.

The storm was still raging. Trees were crashing in the nearby forest.

Mr Bruce, Tom's dad, stood in the doorway of the cottage. He turned to his wife. "I have to go out. The way the trees are falling they could block the road into the forest and, after all, it's my job to keep the road and paths clear."

Tom's mother looked worried. "Are you sure? Can't you wait till morning?"

"I'm afraid I can't. Some of the coaches from the dance will be using the road getting back to Trent. It's only the small branches at the entrance to the forest that have come down, I'm quite sure."

He lit his lantern and made his way to the forest, the wind nearly blowing him off his feet. He shone the lantern. He was right. It did seem that it was some of the smaller trees that had got blown down. They had served as a windbreak for the larger trees.

He went to turn home after clearing the entrance. He swung his lantern round in an arc and got a shock. It picked up a coach that was partly hidden in the trees. He had almost missed it.

When he went closer he noticed that it was black. No wonder he hadn't noticed it. How strange, he thought. But then he decided it must be someone from the dance. He did notice that it was facing towards the London road and the horses were as black as the coach.

He turned once again to go home. Two men ran past, nearly knocking him down. They jumped aboard the coach, shouted at the horses and took off at great speed, not once showing any light.

The coach raced through the village. When they got to the outskirts they stopped to light the lanterns. They set off again but they hadn't gone far when something ran in front of them—some animal, a deer or a dog. It scared the horses. They reared up. The coach ended up in a ditch. When one of the men examined it he found the axel completely buckled. They started to argue about what to do.

"We can't go back to Ralph to tell him about the mess we made of the job he gave us. I'm beginning to think we are working for a madman."

The taller of the two men snarled. "It's all your fault. You didn't have to hit the old lady so hard. We were only supposed to frighten her into telling us who the young girl is and to look for papers."

"Ralph has been going mad since the coach nearly ran that young girl down. Remember, he kept muttering about the girl having a star mark on her neck."

The younger of the two men said, "I remember. That was some night! Ralph went into a funny mood. He couldn't be bothered with the gambling or the women but we partied till the early hours."

"We were onto a good thing bringing the gamblers and women from London once a week to Ralph's big house. I suppose this will be the end of that."

"I suppose we better go back to face the music. If we carry on to London, sure as fate Ralph will find us and if he does, God help us."

The other man agreed. They unhitched the horses and keeping well off the beaten track made their way back to the Howard estate and Ralph.

The dance had come to an end. Everyone was milling around, the ladies fetching their cloaks, everyone admitting that it had been a grand night.

Jessie declined Dr Brown's offer of a lift home. "I just have a few yards to go but as soon as I get it sorted out at home I'll be ready to start work with you."

Dr Brown helped Tansy into the pony trap.

"What a wonderful, wonderful night it's been! I won't be able to get to sleep for ages. I will have to tell Gran-Mere everything."

When they arrived at the cottage they were surprised to find the door open. It was crashing backwards and forwards in the wind.

"Something is wrong!" Tansy shouted, running into the cottage. Dr Brown followed behind.

Gran-Mere was lying on the floor. She was moaning. All around the room drawers were pulled out and papers strewn about the floor. Gran-Mere tried to rise but collapsed on the floor again. There was a cut on the side of her head.

They helped her into her bed. Dr Brown examined her. "I think she has a broken arm but it's her head I am worried about. You know which herbs to use, Tansy, to calm her down. She keeps muttering about two men."

Tansy was busy mixing the herbs to sooth her—lavender to relax her nerves, borage mixed in wine to drive away sadness and basil to prevent her vomiting with shock.

Dr Brown and Tansy sat with her into the night. Tansy thought she had aged as she started to come round fully. She grasped Tansy's hand.

"The two men just came barging in. I was sitting by the fire half asleep. I was waiting for you to come home. They shouted at me: 'Who is the girl staying with you? Where did she come from?' I just shook my head. That made them angry. They started looking for papers. I heard one of them say, 'He told us to find some evidence.' One of them called me an old witch. He punched me so hard that I fell. That's all I remember. I must have passed out."

Tansy, in tears, hugged her. "Oh Gran-Mere, it's all my fault."

"Hush now, child," she said. "For sixteen years you have brought me nothing but happiness."

CHAPTER 17

LATER Gran-Mere slept. In the morning she had got back her old spirit, but overnight she had become an old woman.

"I have got so much to tell you, Tansy, about my years before coming here."

"Not now, Gran-Mere. Please rest and I will tell you all about the dance later."

Gran-Mere looked at her. "You are still wearing your beautiful dress. Oh child, you have sat all night with me. Look, you have stained it."

So Tansy had to tell her about the jealous girl at the dance spilling red wine on her.

"Oh Tansy my darling, watch out for her. She could do you harm, just as someone done me harm many years ago. One day, Tansy, I will tell you my story. You are right—I feel very tired. I think I will sleep now."

The whole village was shocked at the attack on Gran-Mere. There were no police in any of the villages. The gentry governed the country as Justices of the Peace. In Redburn when there was trouble the villagers reported to Sir Edward as justice of the peace.

In no time Sir Edward gathered a group of villagers to search for the two men but they had to give up. They all believed that they had disappeared back to London. Only Tansy, Gran-Mere and Dr Brown knew the truth, but they told no one. The time wasn't safe to let everyone know the truth about Tansy.

The two men stood facing Ralph, his face black with anger at them. The years had not been kind to him. His drinking and debauchery over the years had told on him. "You fools!" he raved. "The coach could be traced back to me. Take some of the men and the blacksmith and get the coach back on the road to London. And leave it locked up in my yard there."

When the men had gone, Ralph stood muttering to himself: "Could it be Kathryn's child?"

The next minute, impossibly, he would convince himself the baby died with Kathryn.

They were buried together.

He went over and over everything in his mind.

"This estate is mine! Michael tried to take it away from me but that was sorted. That old man saying he was my father, wanting money from me—he, too, was sorted. That mark on the girl's neck, it was a Howard birthmark! It appeared on that place for generations." He paced up and down. "I *have* to find out." Then a look of cunning came over his face. "When those two idiots come back from London I have a job for them."

CHAPTER 18

THE two men stared in horror at Ralph. They had arrived back from London a few minutes before.

Ralph was like a madman. The men faced him. "We won't do it!"

They backed towards the door.

Ralph produced a gun from under his cloak. He fired over the men's' heads. "The next time I will maim you for life, with broken knee caps." He bared his teeth. "Oh yes. I will say I caught you both burglaring the house. My word against yours!"

The men stood shaking.

"Now," Ralph continued. "Tonight we are going to the church. We will wait until the early hours. No one is likely to be about and especially near a church. We will only light the lanterns when we are in the church. We will go to the crypt where all the Howards rest and we will find the coffin of Kathryn. It will be beside Michael's. As you know, all the coffins are of heavy stone. We will take tools to open Kathryn's and then we will find out if Kathryn's baby was buried with her."

One of the men started to blubber. "We could be hung for doing it!

One of my mates was hung for stealing a bag of meal."

Ralph snarled at him, "I will hang you myself if there is another word from you."

It was nearly one o'clock in the morning when they set off. It was a moonless night. They left the pony and trap in some trees and crept towards the church. The church door was open. All the church doors in the country were open. The church was there for anyone in need of shelter. People were unlikely to cause damage in a church partly because of the wrath of God and partly because of superstition.

They made their way to the crypt. They found Kathryn's coffin. Ralph, almost dancing with impatience, urged the men on.

"Move it, move it, get the lid off!" he shouted.

♣

Jim, the old miller, making his way home much the worse for drink, was talking away to himself.

"I'll be in trouble when I get home. I have never been home as late as this but, oh, it was a good night drinking with old friends."

As he approached the church he rubbed his eyes. Were those lights flickering at the church windows? "Ach, I must be seeing things." He walked a few more yards but then, again, the lights flickered in the church windows.

He approached the church cautiously, then made his way inside. He saw the lanterns and shadows of three men. They were by the crypt.

Then his blood ran cold. From the crypt came mad laughter and a man shouting: "It's not here, there is no baby here!"

He tried to run out of the church but his legs wouldn't move. Then he was shoved aside as two men ran past him.

The mad laughter went on.

With an effort he moved and ran for his life. He saw the two men disappearing down the road, still running.

He almost collapsed into his wife's arms when he got home. She started to shout at him: "You drunken old fool."

Then she realised that something was wrong with him. He was shaking like a leaf and was babbling on about the church and Satan. She could get no sense out of him. Eventually he crawled into bed.

The next day he wouldn't move from his bed and kept his head under the bedclothes.

She was really worried by this time. She thought he had taken a brainstorm. She asked the minister to visit him because he kept on about the church and the dead.

It took a long time for the minister to get the story from him. "I'll go up to the church," he said. "And check things out."

The first thing they noticed was that the lectern had been knocked over. Prayer books were lying scattered. The crypt was open and then he noticed that Kathryn's coffin lid was partly removed.

Old Jim was right. Something devilish was going on here, but thank God the body was not disturbed. It could have been grave robbers, but from now on the church will be securely locked!

Jim wondered what had happened to the two men who had run in fear from the church—and why was the other man shouting that the baby was not there? It will all come out one day, he thought to himself, but it took a long time before he would venture near the church.

CHAPTER 19

Gran-Mere's Story

GRAN-MERE and Tansy, unaware of the terrible thing that Ralph had done in the church, were trying hard to forget the horror of the attack by the two men. She was sitting propped up in bed, looking old and frail, but there was a determined look on her face.

"Now, Tansy, I want you to take a key from under the herb basin. It will open the caddy that I keep my tea in. As you know, tea is as precious as gold. Just use a few leaves of it to make two cups. Yes, my dear, you may have your first cup of tea." Tansy looked at her in surprise. "I think we both need to be refreshed before I start telling you my story.

"I don't remember when I became known as Gran-Mere. My name is Maria Donettie. My mother was French and my father Italian. They met when my mother visited Italy as a companion to an old English lady. They married and I was born two years later. I can remember how happy they were together.

"I was nine when a terrible disease came to the little village near Naples. It took away half the population including my dear mother and father. It was believed that the disease came in on the ships from the Far East. I was heartbroken."

She stopped talking. Tansy wiped away a tear from her cheek. After a moment she continued.

"I went to live with my grandmother. She was a widow. She lived in a little house in the mountains above Positano. I was happy living with grandmother. I was brought up without anyone my own age, but I was kept busy. We had goats and made cheese which we sold in the market in Positano.

"We had enough ground to grow olives, oranges and lemons. What we didn't use we sold in the market. Grandmother made beautiful lace. It was in great demand by brides and by the churches to trim altar clothes.

"As the years went past grandmother found it too difficult going down the mountain to Positano, so it became my job to go there once a week to the market. I loved going there. I met girls my own age."

Gran-Mere closed her eyes. Tansy thought she had fallen asleep. She bent over her to straighten her pillow, but her eyes flew open. "I'm not asleep, my darling. I will just rest now and then for a few minutes. I have got such a lot to tell you and I feel for my own sake as well as yours, I must finish my story.

"I will talk for a little while longer and I see that darkness is coming and you will have to do your chores. Tomorrow when I am stronger I will continue."

Dr Brown came the next morning to see Gran-Mere. Tansy told him about Gran-Mere telling her story. "I feel that it is taking too much out of her," she said.

Dr Brown smiled at Tansy. "Don't worry, my dear. Gran-Mere is a very determined woman. Let her continue. I know most of her story and I think you should hear it."

When she was ready Gran-Mere took up her story again. "Grandmother had an order for her finest lace. It was for a bride's wedding dress. I packed it carefully and carried it on my back and made my way down the mountain to Positano.

"I think I may have been just as much to blame for what happened. My mind was far away. I was thinking about this girl who would be wearing the beautiful lace on her wedding day. I was at a bend on the road. I hadn't heard the horses until they were on me. I jumped out of their way and landed in a ditch, the bundle of lace spilling out.

"I looked up at the horsemen. There were three of them and one girl. One of the horsemen jumped off his horse and held out his hand to help me up. I thought he was the most handsome man I had ever seen. He towered above me, blue eyed with reddish fair hair.

"'Are you all right, my dear?' He sounded English, but something different in the tone of his voice. The girl spoke to him. 'Do come along, Ian. It was the foolish girl's own fault. She had plenty time to keep clear.'

"The man called. Ian ignored her and he started to pack the lace into the bag. The girl edged her horse closer. With her riding whip she hooked a piece of lace.

"'I will have this, Ian. Could you give the girl some money for it?' I snatched it back. 'I'm sorry, it is not for sale,' I told her.

"'Oh, so the peasant talks English,' she said. I looked at her. She was pretty. Dark hair, beautiful fair skin, but as I looked at her I thought that her mouth spoilt her looks. Her lips as she looked at me were curled into a sneer and when the man called Ian asked me my name, I saw real rage on her face.

"'Goodbye, Maria!' he shouted as they galloped off.

"I remember feeling a bit sad. I would have liked to listen to the man Ian with the strange accent."

CHAPTER 20

"IT was just over a week after the incident with the horsemen. I went to the market in Positano. After I finished selling some produce I decided to visit the church to get a look at the bride who would be wearing my grandmother's lace on her gown.

"I stood well back. I felt so grimy after a day standing at the stall. I felt a hand on my shoulder and a voice that I recognised. It had been going on in my head for over a week. 'Hello Maria.' he said. 'You got over your tumble.' I suddenly felt shy. 'Yes sir,' I had replied. 'Just call me Ian,' he said. He looked at the bride. 'Your grandmother's lace is quite beautiful.' He smiled. 'Now Maria, let me take you for a cool drink. I noticed them selling lemon water in one of the cool courtyards.'

"I had hesitated for only a moment. I felt so comfortable with him. We sat talking for ages. He asked me all about my life and he told me that he came from Scotland. He described the little village he lived in—in the Highlands of Scotland, among the mountains and lochs.

"We were still deep in conversation when a voice said, 'So here you are, Sir Ian!' It was the girl who had been with them on the day of the incident. I had disliked her on that day and when I looked at her I saw in her face her dislike of me.

"Ian turned to me. 'You haven't been properly introduced. This is Fiona Monroe, our travelling companion. We are here to buy wine. We get it shipped back to Scotland along with other things, like oil.'

"It had taken a moment for me to register the fact that she had called him Sir Ian. I was taken aback. I didn't know whether to curtsey to him. Instead, I said a quick goodbye and ran."

Gran-Mere had closed her eyes again. Tansy thought her mind had probably gone back to that day in Positano. She left her and put the water on to make a cup of her precious tea.

When she went back with the tea, Gran-Mere smiled at her. "You are so patient with me, Tansy. I am inclined to ramble a bit. The tea has refreshed me. Can you bear to listen for a bit longer, Tansy?"

"Of course I can, Gran-Mere. Your story is like a fairy tale."

"Not all of it, Tansy, not all of it."

Gran-Mere continued her story.

"June passed and a few months later grandmother died. She was a good age and she just passed away peacefully in her sleep. I missed her terribly. She had always been so kind to me. She taught me so many things. It was from her I got my knowledge of herbs.

"It was a lovely summer evening. I was sitting in the garden. It had been very hot during the day and I was enjoying the evening coolness. My heart jumped when I heard the voice. 'Good evening, Maria Donnettie.' It was Ian. Nearly a year had passed since our last meeting. We shook hands very formally but we both felt this strong feeling between us.

"'I have thought such a lot about you, Maria. I just had to come to see you again,' he said. 'I am going to be in these parts for nearly a year. My people are looking after everything at home. There is a housekeeper. She looked after my father and now she looks after me. Old Donald the gamekeeper and his son, young Donald, they are good honest people. My property will be well looked after when I am away.

"'So Maria, can you spare some time for me to show me the sights of your country?"

"So the happiest time of my life began. I took him to Rome and walked down the Spanish steps to the Trevi fountain. We both made our wishes, throwing coins into it. I know that my wish was to have Ian's company for ever and ever. We went to Pompeii. It was amazing to see all the marks on the granite stones of the chariots two thousand years ago. Some of the crude pictures made me blush and Ian laughed at me.

"A thin tendril of smoke was rising from Vesuvius, the volcano that had destroyed the whole city of Pompeii with the loss of tens of thousands of lives. I was pleased to leave it. There was so much history in and around Rome—it would take a lifetime to visit them all.

"The next day I took Ian to the island of Capri. We visited the blue grotto there. It's a cave that you can only enter when the tide is low. Even sitting in the boat we had to duck our heads to get in. It was huge inside and the reflection of the sea on the rocks turned everything bright blue. It was so beautiful! I held my breath. Ian took my hand and his voice was gentle in my ear. 'I know we have only known each other a short time, but I have fallen in love with you, Maria. Do you think you could love me?'

"I was so happy I thought my heart would burst! I could only nod.

"'I want to marry you, Maria, and take you home with me to Scotland.'

"'Yes, yes, I do love you, Ian.' I remember him kissing me for the first time, surrounded by all the beauty of the blue grotto.

"A few weeks later we were married in a little church in Positano. I wore a simple cotton dress, but my veil was one of the finest of grandmother's lace."

"In fact, Tansy," she said catching her hand. "The lace is in that trunk in the comer. I hope that one day you will wear it on your wedding day."

CHAPTER 21

"GRAN-MERE, I think you have done enough talking for today." Tansy tucked the clothes round her. "Tomorrow, when you are rested, you can continue."

Tansy was worried for her. She wasn't just telling a story, she seemed to be living it. To Tansy, Gran-Mere was always a strong person in mind and body, but each day since the attack by the two men she seemed to be getting weaker. She knew that Gran-Mere was worried for her. She had convinced herself that Ralph knew who she was and was just waiting to do her harm.

The next morning Tansy was up and about early. She had to go to the woods to collect more herbs. She tiptoed from the house. Gran-Mere was sound asleep. She locked the door behind her, something no one in the village had to do before Gran-Mere's attack.

She knew exactly where to go for the herbs she needed. She was only away for less than an hour. As she approached the cottage she saw a man standing at the door. Her heart nearly stopped. She hid behind a bush. The man turned to leave. There was something familiar about him.

Then she gave a scream of delight. It was Tom! She went to hug him. Then, her face flaming with embarrassment, she drew back. This wasn't Tom, her childhood companion, but a young man. He grinned at her and gave her a peck on the cheek.

"Well, well, Tansy. Quite a young lady you are now," he said. "It seems no time since we went to raid apples at Sir Alexander's orchard."

Tansy looked at him. Even the bright red hair had quietened to a reddish brown. He stood nearly a foot above Tansy. Gone was the boy she remembered, until he grinned again and there he was, freckles and eyes full of mischief.

They went in to see Gran-Mere. She was sitting up in bed, a worried look on her face. "Tansy, who were you talking to? Are you all right?"

"Yes, she is quite all right, Gran-Mere, and a lovely young lady she has become." Gran-Mere peered at the man who followed Tansy into the room.

"Oh, Tom Bruce, it's you." She held out her arms to him. "I'm so glad to see you. Why has it taken so long for you to come back?"

"Well, Gran-Mere, to a poor student London is far away. And not only that, I have been to a lot of different parts of England. I have to learn the laws of the country—people as well as the laws of the cities. Dad managed to visit me a few times and mother only once. She hates London." He smiled. "But enough about me, Gran-Mere. I heard about the attack on you. It is becoming a wicked world. It's poverty that is causing a lot of the trouble. London is not a safe place to live. I myself would never walk the streets at night.

"Sir Edward and Lady Frail have been so kind to me. I think I have repaid them by doing so well in all my exams. Do you know they even bought me clothes? They pretended that they belonged to Ian to save my pride. But I knew they were brand new.

"Now Gran-Mere, I must tell you that I am going to finish my final year as a lawyer at your solicitors in London, Young & Dobie."

"That is simply wonderful, Tom. I do a lot of business there, and so does Dr Brown. Instead of us having to go to London, you could come to see us to do business."

Tom smiled. "Sir Alexander is a sly fox. I think that he had already worked all that out when he got me the position at Young and Dobie. I am going back to London tonight, but I hope to be back here soon."

He gave Gran-Mere a hug and Tansy another peck on the cheek and with a wave he was gone.

Gran-Mere and Tansy looked at each other. Now the room seemed empty without him.

Since Gran-Mere and Tansy hade gone to help Tom's parents many years before, Tansy noticed that Gran-Mere had been a frequent visitor to them. She seemed to enjoy their company. This was very unusual. Gran-Mere in all the years that Tansy knew her had never struck up a friendship with anyone.

When Tom had gone Gran-Mere continued with her story.

"Ian was beginning to get impatient. It had been nearly a year since he had left his beloved Scottish Highlands. We stayed for a short time in London. Ian helped me to buy warm clothes because, as he said, it would be September before we arrived in his village, Baldune. Ian spoke of it so often and told me so many stories about it that I was getting just as excited to get there.

"We arrived in Glasgow on a miserable wet afternoon. I was exhausted after so much travelling and Ian, desperate to get home, would not move till I had rested for a few days. Throughout the whole journey he had been so kind and thoughtful.

"The next day we walked about the town and Ian told me some of the history of Glasgow. He showed me with pride the University of Glasgow. It was the second university in Scotland after St Andrews in the north. Many famous people were taught there such as William Hunter, anatomist and surgeon and many, many more. There was a lot of religious intolerance there. It had swept through Europe led by Martin Luther from Germany.

"The buildings were made of timber and thatch and were set close together. I thought they looked like something from a fairytale. When I said this to Ian he laughed. 'Some fairytale!' he said.

"I did change my mind when a pale of slops thrown from a window missed us by inches. We walked by a river—the Clyde, Ian called it. It was a beautiful river filled with boats of all shapes and sizes. Ian explained that a lot of the merchandise he had bought in Italy would be unloaded there.

"We stayed in Glasgow for four days. I was completely rested. We set out for Baldune at dawn.

"It was a lovely morning. We left Glasgow far behind. We stopped for a rest at the most stunning loch. Then, off we set into the most breathtaking countryside. I had never imagined anything like it. Mountains rose each side of the narrow road.

"We passed through a steep gorge. The mountains, covered in purple heather, shone in the evening sun.

"'Oh Ian,' I remember saying, 'I will never forget the magic of this moment.'

"Then I nearly jumped out of my skin. A huge animal was standing near the road looking at us. It had the biggest horns on each side of its head.

"Ian was bent double, laughing. 'Oh Maria, that is a deer, a big stag. It is more frightened of us! I must admit he is a big animal and those horns, as you call them, are antlers. That old fellow is a Royal. He has twelve points on his antlers, which makes him pretty special. I may come across him again when we go hunting.'

"'Oh Ian, you couldn't kill him!' I remember being horrified when Ian explained that they were used as another source of food, called venison. They were good clean animals that lived on the herbs and lichen on the mountains. I had so much to learn of the Scottish Highlands."

CHAPTER 22

"WE looked down this beautiful valley. A loch was shining in the distance. 'That is Loch Munda.' Ian said. 'We will cross it. It's only a short distance to Baldune House and home.'

"We approached the village. Some of the villagers were working in the fields. They just stood and stared as the coach passed. I was getting more and more nervous.

"The houses stretched down the hillside almost to the shore. To me they seemed to blend into the hillside. They were so small with their roofs of thatch and heather. Further along the road were the village inn, shop and a small church.

"Ian stopped the coach at the top of the road. 'We will walk from here, Maria. The village people will want to meet you. The coach with all our baggage will go round the loch.'

"As we approached, the tallest man I have ever seen came to meet us. He had long red hair and a beard so long that it covered his whole chest. I remember Ian was so delighted to see him. They clapped each other on the back. Ian turned to me. 'Maria, this is Dhol Beag. That's Gaelic for wee Donald.' I looked at Ian, puzzled. He had laughed at me. 'Just wait till you meet his father, Dhol Mhor.'

"Donald, this giant of a man, turned to me and with a beautiful soft lilting voice said, 'Welcome, Lady Moncrieff, to Baldune.'

"We followed Donald down the road. The whole village seemed to have come to meet us. They were all silent. A little child of about three stood in the middle of the road as we approached, quite unaware of this man and woman. She proceeded to lift her dress and have a piddle. There was laughter. It broke the ice and soon everyone was crowding round us wishing us welcome.

"A woman pushed a bunch of roses into my arms. 'For you, Lady Moncrieff. I grew them specially for you.'

"Out of the corner of his mouth Donald whispered: 'Stolen from Baldune House, I have no doubt.'

"We had made our way to the boat. I was so happy that the village people had welcomed me when a loud woman's voice shouted from the crowd: 'A pity you couldn't find a wife among your own people, Sir Ian!' Ian ignored her. Someone started to ring a large bell that was fixed to a rock. From across the loch there was an answering bell from Baldune House. It was then that I heard bagpipes, the sound carrying across the loch.

"Ian turned to me. 'Welcome to my country, my darling Maria.' It was all so beautiful."

As Gran-Mere told her story the tears flowed. Tansy insisted that Gran-Mere rested.

"In fact, Gran-Mere, maybe you shouldn't continue your story until you are stronger."

"No Tansy. I want to. You have got no idea the relief it is to me to tell it after so many years."

The next morning Gran-Mere, sitting up in bed, looked so much better.

"Do you know, Tansy? Not in my time but maybe in yours, there will be men policing the villages. They will maybe be something like soldiers. I know that Sir Edward as magistrate is very honest and fair, but some villages are not so fortunate and the men there are supposed to uphold the law. Some of the bailiffs for instance are worse than the people they take to be judged."

Tansy looked at Gran-Mere in surprise. "Now what has brought that on, Gran-Mere?"

"Don't mind me, Tansy. Lying here, my mind is racing hither and thither. I was thinking about some of the poor innocent people who were maybe condemned to death through hatred and jealousy by their fellow men.

"Now, as I see it, if some of the charges were brought by an independent group of men who had nothing to gain through it, we would have fairer justice."

"When you were thinking all these things, Gran-Mere, did something happen in Scotland to you?"

Gran-Mere didn't answer her. Instead, she said, "Come now, Tansy, let me finish my story." She took a deep breath and continued. "The boat took us across Loch Munda. The pipers met us on the shore and piped us through big iron gates and along a short drive to Baldune House.

"How can I describe the house! It was huge, more like a castle. It was built of grey granite, a wing on each side and a large courtyard leading up to the front door. It wasn't a beautiful house. The grey granite made it seem cold, but there was something about the massive strength that made it appealing. One could feel safe there.

"And with all the troubles in the Scottish Highlands, it would stand in good stead.

"Standing at the door was a small man. He had the same red hair and beard as Donald. Ian, with a smile, introduced me to him. 'This is Dhol Mhor, Donald's father. He is called Big Donald.'

"'But Ian…' I spluttered.

"'I know, my dear, this is just a bit of highland humour. The big is small and the small is big.'

"We entered Baldune House through large solid oak doors. The staff were lined up in the entrance hall to welcome us. There was cook, a small stout woman with a happy smiling face who curtsied. 'Welcome, my lady,' she said.

"One by one they were introduced. One young girl of about fourteen was overcome by shyness. She kept her head lowered and it was only when she got a push in the back from another of the servants that she managed to curtsy. I took to her immediately. I asked her her name. 'Hetty,' she said. 'And what do you do, Hetty?' I asked her. 'I am learning to wait on tables, my lady,' she said.

"I looked around the massive room. A large table dominated the room. It was dark oak. It would seat thirty to forty people. There were two large silver centrepieces filled with fruit and flowers.

"The fireplace, as like everything else in this house, was burning brightly with, it seemed to me, nearly a whole tree burning there. At one of the bay windows a table was set. It was set for three. I presumed it was for Ian and I. I looked at Ian, wondering for whom the third place was set. A voice that I recognised and disliked said, 'Welcome home, Ian.' It was Fiona, striding down the hall towards us. She pecked Ian on the cheek.

"Then she turned to me. 'I am sure you must feel like freshening up. One of the maids will take you to your room. Dinner will be at seven.'

"I felt as though I was a guest and she was the mistress. And you, Tansy, know how angry I can get at any unfairness. And I was angry. I turned to her. 'No Fiona, Ian will take me to our room.'

"Donald Mhor, carrying the cases from the coach that had just arrived, winked at me behind Fiona's back and I knew I had a true friend there; in fact, I had taken immediately to the two Donalds.

"The bedroom, as I expected, was huge—a four-poster bed draped in faded blue velvet. A large bay window overlooking the loch had the same faded curtains. A fire was burning brightly, sending a warm glow into the room. I remember Ian laughing at me when I said I could get lost in the big bed.

"'Oh, but Maria, I would soon find you,' he said, tossing me as though I was a feather onto the bed.

"I opened one of the trunks looking for something to wear.

"'What about one of the suits you bought in London?' Ian reminded me. He was right. I put on a soft woollen suit. It was a lovely blue colour. I remember being horrified at what it had cost

"We made our way down the wide staircase to dinner. Fiona was waiting for us. The first night in Ian's home I would have loved it to have been just the two of us having our first meal there. Fiona almost ignored me at the table, talking business with Ian until he turned, squeezed my hand and said to Fiona. 'Enough business talk. We don't want to bore my lovely wife, do we?'

"Fiona flushed scarlet and glared at me.

"Looking back, it always surprised me that Ian never once realised the dislike Fiona had for me. And as time went on the dislike turned to hatred."

Once again Gran-Mere's eyes closed. Telling her story in her weakened condition was putting a strain on her.

She slept for some time. Tansy managed to get some work done in the house. They had two goats that had to be milked. She decided to bake some scones. She had just finished when there was a shout. It was Tom's father. He had a load of firewood in his cart. He piled them up neatly at the end of the cottage.

"How is Gran-Mere?" he asked when he came in.

"She will love to see you. I will set a tray with some scones and milk. We can have it in with Gran-Mere."

Gran-Mere, looking better after her sleep, was delighted to see him and asked all about what was happening in the village. She was especially interested in the news of Tom. She was delighted to hear that he would be coming to Redburn soon. She continued her story after Tom's visit.

"Now, Tansy, where was I? Oh yes… When we finished dinner, Dol Mhor came in. He drew Ian aside and spoke softly to him. Once again Fiona looked angry. She turned to Ian. 'I will show Maria round the house tomorrow morning. I will stay tonight.'

"'No need,' said Ian. 'I want to show her her new home myself and I have a surprise for her in the morning.'

"Dol Mhor turned to Fiona. 'I have pulled the boat up for you, Fiona. It's ready for you to row across.' Once again Dol Mhor winked at me.

"Fiona had no excuse to stay.

"In the morning Ian showed me round the house. It was so big! One wing wasn't used. It was full of very dark furniture. I felt that the whole house needed new drapes and carpets.

"Then on the ground floor he showed me into a room. 'This was my mother's room,' he said, opening the door.

"It took my breath away. It was so beautiful. The first impression was that it was full of sunshine. There were couches and pretty little chairs scattered throughout the room covered in pale yellow brocade. A carpet of the softest green matched the curtains. The room had a delicate air to it. It was more French than Scottish. The tall windows opened to an amazing garden. A little burn ran through it. Stepping stones across led to a little summerhouse. Hollyhocks were growing up the walls. Along the side of the burn were masses of plants, some still in bloom.

"The rose garden reached through two or three trellises and was still full of flowers.

"'Oh Ian!' I exclaimed. I was so happy. I remember hugging him. He said: 'This room and garden were my mother's pride and joy. The room has kept its colour because when mother died the blinds were brought down. Dol Mhor and Dol Beag look after the garden. I knew you would love it. It will be your own special room.'

"And indeed it did become that. I think it was that room that kept me sane."

"'Come now,' Ian had said. 'You must see your surprise.' He took me outside to the yard. Dol Mhor was holding a beautiful white horse by the reins. 'Oh, she is beautiful!' I exclaimed, stroking her nose. I noticed she was quite young.

"Ian and Dol Mhor were smiling. 'So you like my present to you?' Ian had said. 'I remember you telling me that your father had taught you to ride as a child.'

"I couldn't speak. I was bursting with happiness. I just hugged him.

"Just then Fiona appeared. 'Well, well, a close kept secret.' She was looking at Dol Mhor. She turned to me. 'Quite a change from the donkey you used to ride.'

"But nothing she could say or do could take away the happiness of that whole day.

"'What will you call her?' Ian asked. I looked at the beautiful white horse. 'I think I will call her Lilly.' Over the years I grew to love my Lilly.

CHAPTER 23

"LIFE went on for me in that beautiful Highland village," Gran-Mere continued. "Ian and I rode for miles over the estate. The air was so pure, the hills changing from day to day. Sometimes he would have to leave Baldune for weeks at a time to do his buying.

"He explained to me that even though the estate was a wealthy one, one needed to have some security. And it was his father who realised this when some of the neighbours lost their estates to the crown. One of them had been Fiona's father. He managed to save enough to buy the inn and shop, but Ian sensed that there was a lot of bitterness in him.

"The two Donalds were great company for me when Ian was away. They had so many stories. It was Dol Beag who told me the story of the Monroes. Apparently Fiona's grandfather and great grandfather were disliked in the area. When there was trouble they jumped from side to side. There was no loyalty in them, only greed. But they lost in the end, losing their estate.

"The great grandfather was the worst. He employed a young boy of thirteen to work in the stables. Apparently he was very cruel to him. He was half starved. He was found eating the hens' food. Not a day passed without him getting a beating.

"The poor child could take no more. He jumped off the rocks and drowned in the loch. Something else he was responsible for.

"'Oh, no more Dol Beag!' I had said to him, but he continued. He told of a young girl that lived alone in one of the village cottages. She earned her living spinning the wool and knitting things to sell.

"'Well, story has it that the great grandfather wanted that cottage. It had a good bit of ground around it. He started to tell the village people all sorts of lies about her and that she was a witch. Eventually the superstitious villagers led by Monroe tied her up and took her to the middle of the loch and threw her in. And of course no one was brave enough to do anything when he took over the cottage.

"'Ian's great grandfather was away when all that had happened. He was leading his men at war. But through the generations there was always a bit of ill feeling between the Monroes and the Moncriefs. That is, of course, until the last number of years. Ian and Fiona grew up together and Fiona's father made a point of being very friendly to Ian.

"'You must know, Maria, that Fiona expected to marry Ian, but as you will have noticed, he just regards her as a friend. There were great sighs of relief when Ian married you. Oh yes, Maria, my Lady, they do love you.'

"I remember feeling so warm and cared for.

"Looking out of the bedroom window one morning, I was surprised and excited to see the snow on the mountains. A few flakes started to fall and in no time the ground had a thin covering; but by afternoon it was covering the ground in two or three inches.

"It was like a winter wonderland outside, the branches of the trees weighed down with snow, Loch Munda shining like a jewel as the snow-covered mountain kissed its shores. From Baldune village shouts of joy came from the children as they played in the snow, the sound coming across the loch in the stillness the snow brought.

"Ian joined me at the door. We stood watching the servants. They were like children, throwing snowballs at each other. Dol Beag had joined them. Even cook had left her kitchen.

"Suddenly a snowball hit Ian on the chest. Well, before you could say one, two, Ian and I had joined them. We were having glorious fun pelting everyone and getting pelted.

"Fiona, coming round the corner of the house, was unfortunate. She got a snowball full in the face. That put an end to the game. She was absolutely furious! One by one the servants crept back into the house.

"Ian and I took her into the house and apologised to her. She was still fuming. 'It was done deliberately!' she shouted. 'I'm going back home.' And we knew that before the day was out everyone in the Highlands would hear about Sir Ian Moncrief and his Italian wife playing with the servants in the snow. And, of course, she would be blaming me."

Tansy looked at Gran-Mere. She had her eyes closed but she was smiling. Tansy realised once more that Gran-Mere, telling her story, was reliving it.

She hoped that Gran-Mere's story would continue to be happy memories because she didn't think that in her weakened state she could cope with bad ones.

While Gran-Mere slept Tansy took the chance of going to the village shop. She was just leaving, her arms full of groceries, her head bent, when she bumped into someone. "You have a big load there, Tansy," a voice said. She looked up. It was Ian.

"Let me help you, Tansy. How have you been?" He walked with her to the cottage. "I was sorry to hear about Gran-Mere but she is a strong woman. She will be fine, I'm sure."

The tears started to run down Tansy's cheeks. "Oh, Ian, she is no longer a strong woman. I am so worried about her."

He put the shopping down and put his arms around her. And that is what Eva Williams saw as she came down the road.

Ian greeted her. "Oh, hello, Eva. Have you been up to the house?"

"Yes, your mother and father have just arrived from London. They sent me to look for you."

"Oh well, I better go. Will you be all right, Tansy?"

"Yes, Ian, I'll be fine."

Eva just looked daggers at her.

"Tell Gran-Mere I'll be up to see her," Ian shouted as they parted.

Tansy hurried home. She was glad to see Ian but she felt upset at Eva's animosity. When she told Gran-Mere what had happened, Gran-Mere hugged her. "I think you will have to be careful with that young lady. I have told you that already. It was someone like her that ruined my life." She smiled. "Is it not strange, Tansy, that your good friend should be called Ian and that my husband was Ian? I think it is a special name for special men. Did you ever wonder, Tansy, why, from all the wide world, that I should choose to live here in Redburn and that Sir Edward should have befriended us? Well, strange as life is, Ian's father and Sir Edward met when they were both young men touring in France. They became good friends and I believe Sir Edward visited Baldune on many occasions.

"Ian was the family name of the Moncriefs and when Sir Edward and Lady Frail had a baby boy, they called him Ian, remembering their friendship. I don't think my Ian Moncrief and Ian Frail ever met.

"It had stuck in my mind, Ian talking about this little village called Redburn, and Sir Edward, so when my wanderings took me here many, many years later, I looked up Sir Edward. Both he and lady Frail were so kind. It was them that found me this cottage." She sighed. "I am so sorry Tansy, I seem to be wandering with my story."

"Gosh," Tansy said. "What a strange thing and so terribly interesting. Does Sir Edward know my story?"

"Not at all!" Gran-Mere's voice was fierce. "Only Dr Brown knows and that's the way I want it to stay for a little while longer."

A few days afterwards Ian called to see Gran-Mere. He sat with Tansy beside her bed.

"As you both know, I have been travelling abroad. I couldn't settle into anything but for a long time now my mind has been made up. I want to go into the medical profession as a doctor or in the long term a surgeon. I have enrolled at Glasgow University. They have now got a worldwide reputation as being far advanced in progressive medicine."

Gran-Mere and Tansy were both thrilled for him.

"I know you will do well in whatever you do," Gran-Mere said.

Ian turned to Tansy. "I know you have been helping Dr Brown. Do you think that Dr Brown would let me go along just to learn the basics first hand?"

Tansy said: "I'm sure Dr Brown would be delighted in the path you want to take."

Just then Dr Brown's pony and trap pulled up. He was on his weekly visit to Gran-Mere. When Ian approached him Dr Brown shook his hand.

"I will be delighted to take you on my rounds," he said.

So it was settled.

CHAPTER 24

GRAN-MERE settled back on her pillows. She had enjoyed the visitors but it had tired her out.

Tansy left her to rest to go and cook a meal. She was always trying to think of different things to whet her appetite and she wanted to think about Ian and Eva.

By evening Gran-Mere wanted to continue her story.

"Christmas Day arrived and all the staff from Baldune House took the boats across the loch to a short service in the village. It was so different from all the Christmas celebrations in Italy.

"Then when New Year's Day came things were different. The wing of the house was opened for the first time in years and on Hogmanay the house was bursting at the seams. I hadn't realised that Ian had so many friends. They kept arriving from some of the neighbouring estates. They came to stay for two or three days.

"The huge table was resplendent. The silver shining, all the beautiful crystal brought out. Cook had some of the village women to help. Little

Hettie forgot to be nervous, she was so excited by it all.

"Ian was wonderful. He was always near me. After all, I was the new bride. I think I played my part well and I passed the test of being Lady Moncrief.

"I was also happy that Fiona was not there to take away my confidence. When I asked Ian why she wasn't there he looked puzzled by my question. 'Fiona helps me with business and she is very good at helping about the house, but she is not part of our social life.'

"Oh Tansy, I could have hugged him! If she only knew what Ian really thought of her. But if I had only known that Fiona was at her worst and most dangerous if she thought that Ian was out of her reach...

"The year went on and soon the summer arrived in a burst of glory in the garden. I spent such happy hours there.

"One hot day in August Ian got cook to make up a picnic for us and we rode to a sheltered beach round the headland. We had the most wonderful day. We swam and splashed about in the sea. Cook had packed a lovely lunch basket and a bottle of Ian's favourite wine. After lunch we lay on the warm sand and Ian talked about his childhood. He had a happy one. I could tell by the way he spoke about it. He didn't seem to miss being an only child.

"His father had a young sister, Jessica, Ian remembered. They used to go exploring, she looking for plants and he looking for birds' eggs. She would never allow him to take more than one from a nest.

"'Where is she now?' I asked him. 'Did she die?'

"He had a troubled look on his face.

"'I don't know,' he said. 'She just disappeared. I think there was a family row. Mother and father never spoke about her. I was very young but there were bits of conversation I overheard. I think she went off to England with some man who worked on the estate. There was talk of her having a child.

"Strange, I haven't thought about her for years and, you know, I could find out what had happened by asking Dhol Mhor. But even if he knew he wouldn't want to discuss it with me. As Dhol Mhor would say, 'Servants don't discuss family matters with their superiors. We know our place.'

"I remember, then, Fiona not being invited to the big celebration at New Year. Aristocrats could go to a dance in the village hall and be made welcome. But unless they were very special village friends, they were not invited as guests to Baldune House.

"I suppose this happened the world over. It is of course snobbery to me. Coming from a little Italian village I couldn't understand it until Ian explained. 'What if we became so friendly with, for instance, the villagers, and had them to stay in Baldune House? How could we hand them a spade next morning and ask them to dig ditches on the estate?' Put so simply by Ian, I did understand

"The wonderful day was coming to an end. The sun had disappeared into the sea in a burst of golden glory. We started to pack away the picnic things when our attention was drawn to the sea. It had been so calm. But now, near the shore, there seemed to be some sort of turmoil. There was a lot of thrashing about.

"Then, along the length of the shore, there was the most strange light near the water's edge. It seemed to have a greenish glow. I had clung to Ian, really afraid. He was all excited. 'It's all right, Maria.' He ran to the loch edge, pulling me along, and *there* was the reason for the light: hundreds, if not thousands, of tiny minute fish were washed up there. And it was the phosphorus element in them that was glowing.

"I remember Ian, still excited about it, explaining to me. 'The mackerel fish, always hungry, must have come across a shoal of what we call shale or minnows. In escaping they landed on the shore,' he went on. 'I remember my father talking about it. He had only seen it once and now I have. Isn't it wonderful that I should see it with the woman I love!'"

Once again Tansy wiped the tears from Gran-Mere's cheeks.

"Oh Tansy, Tansy, how could I have become so bitter that I could forget the great memories that Ian and I had shared?"

Tansy tried to comfort her. "But Gran-Mere, you were so young."

"That was no excuse," she said. "Let me finish my story, then you can judge."

But Gran-Mere slept and the telling of her story was left till the next day.

Ian arrived the next morning with Dr Brown.

"I will be glad of his help," the Doctor said. "I am missing your help, Tansy." He looked in on Gran-Mere. When he came out he was shaking his head.

"I am worried about her, Tansy. She doesn't seem to be improving. Is she still talking about her past?"

When Tansy nodded, he said, "Well, she is so determined. There is nothing we can do about it. She seems to want you to hear it all. And everything Gran-Mere does, it's for a reason."

The next morning, to Tansy's surprise when she went into Gran-Mere's room, she found her sitting by the bed. She had washed and dressed and was busy brushing her hair.

"Don't look so surprised, Tansy. I am feeling much stronger today and if you could manage, I would like you to ask Tom's mother to come and visit me. You and Dr brown are so kind, but I would enjoy talking to another woman. Maybe you could make some scones to take with our cup of tea?"

So Tansy, after finishing the housework, went to see Tom's mother. When she told her that Gran-Mere had invited her to tea she seemed surprised but said she would love to visit her.

When she arrived that afternoon Tansy took her straight into Gran-Mere who was still up, sitting by the bed.

Tansy went to sit down beside Tom's mother.

"Haven't you got things to do, Tansy? You were going to make some scones, and aren't the goats due to be milked?"

Tansy knew she had been dismissed and she felt quite hurt. All day Gran-Mere's mood had been strange.

CHAPTER 25

WHEN Tansy brought in the tea later on they hardly seemed to notice her. They were in deep conversation.

When Tom's mother left, Gran-Mere, looking exhausted, went back to bed. But later that afternoon she wanted to continue her story. Tansy wanted to refuse to sit and listen. She still felt hurt by Gran-Mere's attitude that afternoon, but by now her story had started to intrigue, her.

Gran-Mere settled back on her pillows.

"Sometimes I think I loved Ian too much. Maybe it's the Italian and French blood in me." She smiled at Tansy and patted her hand. "You can be hurt too easily, Tansy."

Tansy thought, 'Gran-Mere can see through people so easily. She knew I was hurt.'

"Well," Gran-Mere continued, "after our lovely, unforgettable day at the beach, I started to get things done in the house. I went with Ian to Glasgow. We ordered new curtains and carpets. Dhol Mhor and Dhol Beag helped with the heavy cleaning and I felt that the house was really my home.

"I seldom went to the village. Cook did most of the ordering but when I went to the Monroe's shop to buy little things to take when I went visiting some of the village women, I could tell that Fiona's father could barely be polite to me.

"He had the village people in the palm of his hand. They all owed him money for groceries that they would pay when they got their wage at the end of each month.

"Sometimes the villagers would take their horses and carts and go to the small garrison town about twenty miles away to buy their provisions. This angered the Monroes and he always found a way to punish them. Little things like dropping the salt bag into the sugar bag or a lot of chaff in their oatmeal sack.

"The village women told me all this when I visited them. I couldn't do anything about it. I didn't want to upset Ian by telling him.

"The months and even the first two years at Baldune went by so quickly. It was so wonderful. The snow-tipped mountains in Winter. The yellow gorse and bright green grass in Spring, covered with bluebells. The Summer with the wild roses in the hedgerows. And then the Autumn! All the trees in their reds and golds, the hills covered in purple heather.

"The September moon—Ian called it the hunter's moon, shining on Loch Munda.

"How could anyone not love these Scottish Highlands, so wild but so beautiful!

"It was over two years since Ian and I married and I was becoming desperate to have a baby. Fiona, when she visited Baldune House, would make a point of staring at my stomach and smirking. Ian, bless him, said nothing, but he was the last of the Moncrieffs and I knew he needed an heir.

"One of the kindly village women said to me one day when I held her baby for a moment, 'Your baby will come when you stop feeling anxious about it.'

"I was becoming quite good at picking up their Gaelic language. Years before, in Ian's grandfather's time, no English was spoken, and when a retired minister came to visit him he persuaded him to stay for a year to teach English to the children. And it worked. Because the children spoke it and they taught the parents.

"There was a story about Dhol Mhor. The Monroes had a slaughterhouse in the village and every four months he got a man in to butcher a cow. Dhol Mhor's mother sent him to the slaughterhouse to ask the man for a cow's tongue, a great delicacy. Now Dhol Mhor's mother and Dhol Mhor had no English and the man in the slaughterhouse had no Gaelic, so he hadn't any idea what Dhol Mhor wanted. In the end, not to be beaten, Dhol Mhor shouted at him, 'I want a cow's speaker!'

"Good old Dhol Mhor. I believed every word of it!"

"When the Spring came the village was almost deserted. All the women and children took off into a shieling in the mountains. Everything went—the cattle, nearly all the livestock, their spinning wheels.

"The shieling was in a valley lush with new grass. All sorts of shelters were built. Everyone loved it when the time came every year to go there. A big fire was built in the middle of the shelters and in the evening there would be singing and story telling round it.

"Ian explained it all to me. The livestock were taken so that they would not go near any of the field where the planting was growing, wheat, barley, oats.

"The men did not go with the women. They were all left to look after the fields.

"I asked Ian to take me but he wouldn't hear of it. The women would chase me, he said. 'No men are allowed, but I will take you to the entrance of the valley and you can find your way from there.' He looked a bit dubious. 'I don't know if Lady Moncrieff will be welcome there.' But as usual I was determined and I got my way.

"The shieling was unbelievable! A whole village had been transported into the hills. A burn ran down the side of the dwellings, a lot of them made of stone. They would be used every year. There were shouts of joy from the children as they ran about in the burn. I'm sure it must have been very cold but it didn't seem to bother them. A big fire had already been laid ready to light in the evening.

"When I approached the women came to welcome me. A cup of

milk and a bannock were placed in my hand. 'You can have a meal with us later round the fire,' they said. And indeed there was a lovely smell of cooking coming from the dwellings.

"It was all so wonderful and so natural. And true to their word, when the evening got chilly, the fire was lit and a large pot of lamb stew was placed on bricks beside it and everyone helped themselves. The children dipped large chunks of new bread into the gravy.

"Then one of the women with two children clinging to her skirt started to sing. The rest of the women joined in.

"I would have liked to have stayed but it was beginning to get dark and I had to go. One of the women took me to the valley entrance. Ian was waiting for me there. I took his arm and we walked to the boat. But for all the world I would have loved to have stayed there. When I said this to Ian he reminded me of how wet, cold and miserable it could be in the mountains.

"But I don't think that would have bothered me. It was the closeness and companionship of all the women. Their kindness to each other. They had so little but in a way they had so much.

"It was into my fourth year of marriage that I discovered I was going to have a baby. What joy in Ian's face when I told him! I was three months pregnant. Everyone was so happy. Old Dhol Mhor had tears in his eyes as he shook my hand.

Fiona came to see me. She was so nice! 'You must look after yourself,' she said. She had brought me fruit and sat with me for a while in the garden most days.

"Ian had arranged for a doctor from one of the Glasgow hospitals to come and stay until the baby was born. And afterwards a midwife would come.

"The doctor was a fussy little man who got on everyone's nerves. He drove cook mad, telling her how to cook the meals for me, but Ian said that he was recommended as a very clever doctor.

"I was five months pregnant. I couldn't settle to anything. The doctor wouldn't allow me to do anything in the garden. I wandered down to the stable. Poor Lilly. She was missing all the riding we had done every day. The fussy doctor wouldn't allow it.

"I was stroking Lilly's nose when Fiona appeared.

"'You are really missing riding, aren't you, Maria?'

"When I agreed, she said, 'I just don't understand what harm it would do if you had a gentle ride. Look Maria, I saw the doctor heading for the pier with his fishing rod. He will be out of the way for a while. Why don't you have just a little ride? It will cheer you up.'

"Fool that I was, I agreed.

"Fiona always kept her riding things in the stable. When she visited she would have the use of one of the horses. I left her to saddle up while I went to change in the house. I was so looking forward to riding Lilly.

"There was no one around when we set off riding slowly towards one of the woodland paths. But Lilly seemed unhappy. She was shuddering and she started to toss her head. It was so unusual. She was normally so placid.

"I thought that it was because no one had been on her back for a while. Fiona had gone on ahead. I started to canter after her. Lilly gave a squeal as though in pain and reared up. I can remember falling and then nothing. I must have hit my head. The terrible pain in my stomach brought me round and then it went on, pain after pain. I shouted and shouted for Fiona. Where had she gone? How long had I been lying there?

"Then the blood started to come from me. I was going to lose my baby. Fiona suddenly appeared. 'What has happened? I thought you were just behind me.' I yelled at her to get the doctor. She galloped off. She was away a long time. By the time the doctor arrived I had lost my baby.

"I found out afterwards that if the doctor had been there even an hour earlier the baby might have been saved.

"Where had Fiona been when I had been thrown? And why had it taken so long to get the doctor? He was only ten minutes away at the pier.

"Lilly had galloped back to the stable. She was in a state, foaming at the mouth. Dhol Mhor had quietened her down. She kicked out when he went to remove the saddle. A bit of barbed wire was sticking in her back. The blood was pouring from her. When I had started her trotting the poor beast must have been in agony.

"A lot of questions had to be answered but I was too far gone to know anything. I think I had a breakdown.

"I spent weeks in my yellow sunshine room. I even slept on one of the couches. Sometimes during the night when I couldn't sleep, I would wander into the garden. I went over and over the events of that day.

"Dhol Mhor took great pride in keeping the stables clean and tidy. Where could the barbed wire have come from? And only that morning he had polished the saddle and groomed Lilly. Ian's father would never allow barbed wire on any of the boundaries, nor would Ian. It was such a cruel thing to see any animal caught in it. All the boundaries on the estate were walls and sometimes just hedging.

"The thoughts went round and round in my head. Why was Fiona so keen that I should ride that day? She was the one who saddled Lilly.

"Dhol Beag in his own quiet way had found out that Fiona's father had been fencing in a bit of his ground after having a row with one of the villagers, saying that sheep had been allowed to wander on it. He had been using barbed wire to fence it."

CHAPTER 26

TANSY, more and more shocked as Gran-Mere's story went on, took her hand.

"Did Fiona come to visit you afterwards, Gran-Mere?"

"She did not, but she came to the stable to pick up her saddle and Dhol Beag escorted her forcefully to her boat.

"In all this time I treated Ian so badly. I wouldn't share his bed, not even the bedroom. He was suffering as much as me. I should have been able to comfort him.

"One night he stayed away all night. I was in the garden in the early hours of the morning. I saw him come in. He just looked at me. He never spoke. He went straight to his bedroom.

"A few days afterwards I heard a lot of shouting and yelling in the yard. I opened the window. Dhol Mhor and Dhol Beag were struggling with a woman, trying to drag her away from the house. I didn't recognise her at first. She was yelling like a mad woman. It was Fiona. She looked up and saw me at the window. She was yelling at me.

"'Lady Moncrieff, some Lady! Just an Italian bitch that couldn't give Ian a child! Well, Lady Moncrieff, your dear husband shared my bed three night ago, so you can continue denying him yours!'

"The Donalds pulled her away, still yelling. Something snapped in my head. I ran from the house. I wanted to get hold of her, to put my hands round her throat to silence her forever. I ran to the shore and into the loch to reach her but the boat was too far away from the shore and she rowed away, laughing her evil laugh.

"Dhol Beag carried me back to the house. Cook made me a hot drink and helped me out of my wet clothes. She placed a warming pan between the sheets. I don't know what cook had put in my drink, but I slept. Maybe it was through sheer exhaustion.

"Early in the morning Ian came in to see me. I remember noticing that he looked quite ill. I turned my back on him."

"'Maria, don't do this. Please talk to me. I swear I did not sleep with her. I went to the inn. I was so unhappy. I got very drunk. Mr Monroe would not let me row across the loch. He put me to bed. I didn't know it was Fiona's bed he put me in. I don't even know if it was done on purpose, but I swear I did not sleep with her.'

"I was still so hurt and so angry. I yelled at him: 'You went to see the Monroes, Ian! You drank, I suppose, with Fiona, the woman who killed our baby! I don't want anything more to do with you or Baldune house. I am leaving. I am going back to Italy.'

"I will never ever forget the look of pain and suffering on his dear face, and even then, seeing this, when he bent to kiss me I turned my face away."

Gran-Mere started to cry. Not like before, gentle tears running down her cheeks, but heartbreaking sobs that shook her frail body.

Tansy held her close, desperately wanting to do something to help her.

She quietened after a while. Tansy remembered some of Gran-Mere's herbal medicine. Rosemary and Lilly of the Valley brewed in a little brandy. She had given it to a woman who was grieving for her dead husband. She set about making it; then she spooned it into Gran-Mere. It seemed to work, for after awhile she went into a deep sleep.

Surely, Tansy thought, this story of Gran-Mere must come to an end soon. It was taking too much out of her.

Dr Brown called the next day.

"I have got to talk to you and Gran-Mere. I am just back from Trent but I won't trouble you about it today. I will call tomorrow. Meantime, Tansy, I would suggest that you rest. I think you are feeling the strain of looking after Gran-Mere and listening to her story."

Dr Brown was right. Tansy was desperately wanting to have a few hours to herself, even to walk to the village and talk to people her own age.

Gran-Mere was sitting up when Tansy took water and towels into her room. Tansy washed her face and hands. Gran-Mere smiled at her.

"Now Tansy, you will fetch my clothes. I have had enough of bed. I feel so much stronger."

Tansy was amazed. Had Gran-Mere heard Dr Brown talking? But she couldn't have. Her bedroom door was closed and they had been talking in the kitchen.

Many times something like this would happen. It was as though she could see into people's heads.

"I will finish my story tonight, Tansy. A great weight has been taken from my heart by telling it. You go now, Tansy. Have a walk to the village and maybe bring something nice for tea from the shop."

It was a beautiful day. Tansy enjoyed the sun on her face as she strolled to the village. The women were all out in the sunshine hanging out washing or beating their rugs. They all called out to her as she passed.

She bought some cakes and cured ham, which she knew Gran-Mere liked.

She walked slowly back along the road, not wanting to go back to the cottage and leaving the lovely sunshine behind. She sat on a rock at the side of the road. She took off her bonnet and pulled the pins from her hair. She closed her eyes. She felt quite drowsy.

"Well, what have we here? I think it might be a mermaid with that long hair."

She opened her eyes. Tom was standing beside her. Still half asleep, she stretched up her hand to him.

"Come and sit by me, Tom." She smiled up at him." It's so good to see you."

"Oh, I don't think so," a women's voice said. "Tom and I have plans for the day." Tansy sat up quickly. It was Eva. She had her arm tucked possessively in Tom's.

Tansy tried frantically to tuck her hair back into some order under her hat. "When did you come home, Tom?" Tansy, bright red with embarrassment, asked him.

"Only this morning. I got a lift with Sir Edward and Lady Frail and Eva decided to come as well. We are on our way to meet Ian. You know he is at home for a while? I have got to see Gran-Mere again—there is something important she wants to discuss with me. How is she? Will it be all right if I call this evening?"

Before Tansy could reply Eva turned to Tom. "What a good idea. I could come with you. I would like to meet this Gran-Mere you are always talking about."

"Sorry Eva, I will be talking private business. Maybe another time."

"Could you maybe leave your business till tomorrow, Tom? We are expecting a visit from Dr Brown."

"Okay, Tansy, that's fine with me. I am going to be here for a few days."

They went off, Eva still holding his arm, smiling up at him.

Tansy felt upset. The sun had gone down but she didn't know why she should suddenly feel so miserable.

When Tansy got home Gran-Mere was sitting at the kitchen table. She looked so much like the old Gran-Mere. Tansy was delighted and when she told her that Tom was coming to see her the next day, she was so excited and happy for the first time in days.

CHAPTER 27

D R BROWN arrived that night. He was looking grave.

"Since I spoke to Tansy yesterday I have been to Trent village."
He was shaking his head. "How can one man cause such distraction? But that is what Ralph has done and is continuing to do."

He turned to Tansy. "Many times I have visited the big house when your grandmother and grandfather lived there and then when it belonged to your lovely mother and father. It was such a delight. The house and the whole estate kept in perfect condition. The barn where your mother and father first danced together at the harvest dance, you could have eaten off the floor. The same with all the outbuildings.

"The workers' cottages were the same. Not a tile was out of place on the roofs. They would be lime-washed and painted every two years. In fact, the whole Howard estate was an example for miles around.

"I am so sorry, Tansy. It has been so run down that even were you to take over the estate tomorrow it would never be the same.

"I had been called in to attend to one of Ralph's friends who had fallen from his horse. His leg was badly broken, showing the bone. He was in a great deal of pain. He wasn't even in a bed. He was left lying on the floor and the only reason Ralph called me in was because the man's screams were getting on his nerves.

"Ralph was lolling about in a chair blind drunk. I have never seen such a change in a man. His face was swollen and debauched looking. He had grown fat.

"The beautiful lounge looked as if animals now lived there. Everything smelt of decay.

"I went to the inn and spoke to some of the old village people. Some of them had worked all their lives on the estate.

"Tansy, I am sorry to have to tell you this. It's a terrible story." He proceeded to tell them about the night her mother's coffin had been opened and the shouts of the man saying the baby wasn't here and the mad laughter from the man.

Gran-Mere's face paled. She held on to the table for support.

"I knew it! I felt danger the last few weeks. It was Ralph. He had to prove whether you were Kathryn's daughter. He suspected when he saw the star on your neck. He is completely mad. He has an obsession about the estate. He will try to kill you, Tansy."

The three of them sat in silence, Tansy and Gran-Mere too shocked to speak.

Then Gran-Mere's strength came to the fore. "Now, Dr Brown, you already know my story. You may stay if you wish, but now I want to tell Tansy the final part. You will know why when I finish. Go now, Tansy. We will all have tea." She smiled a weak smile. "Make it in the teapot. We might have the luxury of two cups each. It could be a long night."

It was indeed a long night. Dr Brown stayed. He wanted to be close in case Gran-Mere collapsed.

The next day Gran-Mere continued her story. "I must finish it, it's important.

"Ian left the house that morning. I watched him talking to Dhol Beag. He was dressed for climbing the mountains. He told me once that when he was in the mountains he always felt peaceful.

"I remember when I was looking at him that day I felt so full of love for him. I had even started to go to him when the memory of Fiona rushed into my mind and I was caught between love and hate for him.

"He waved as he went towards the boat. He would pick up a pony and trap in the village to take him to the mountains.

"I prowled around the house all day. I had such a strange feeling of waiting for something to happen. Late in the afternoon the dogs started to howl and from across the loch the dogs in the village joined in. Dhol Mhor tried to stop them. They would for a moment and then start up again.

"The hair on the back of my neck stood up.

"Dhol Mhor came into the house. 'I'm a bit worried about Sir Ian, he should be coming home now.'

"I remember saying to him it's still light, give him a little more time. But Dhol Mhor insisted. He rowed off to the village. The dogs were still howling.

"The village people had all gathered in a group to meet Dhol Mhor. Their highland instinct had told them something was far wrong. The dogs had sensed it. He spoke to them. 'Get your horses. I'm going to look for Sir Ian.'

"They rode into the glen and near where Sir Ian's favourite climb was they saw his pony and trap. They started to search.

"They found his broken, dead body lying below the ledge where he had fallen.

"I was in the house when the bell from the village sounded. I had learned all the different sounds of the bell—the happy sound for celebrations and the sad sound for death. And this was the sad, ponderous sound for the dead and I knew that it was tolling for Ian.

"Don't ask me how I knew. And when his body, his dear, dear body was brought home across the loch, I was on the shore waiting.

"Is there something in the human body that can only take so much heart pain and all feeling goes from it? Or is it only getting the body used to the terrible anguish to come? I don't know, because from the time of seeing his body taken from the boat an icy coldness took over my mind.

"I made the arrangements for the large dining table to be covered in white sheets and his coffin to be laid there. It was left open so that all could pay their last respects.

"For two days and two nights someone sat by the coffin.

"On the third day it was carried shoulder high to the Moncrieff cemetery. A Moncrieff tartan plaid was laid over the coffin. I followed the slow steps of the piper to Ian's last resting place.

"In the early morning before anyone was awake I went to his grave. I was kneeling there praying when the sun rose above Ian's beloved mountains. The first rays rested on his grave. It was like a last message from him."

"Three days after the funeral I was sitting with Dhol Mhor and Dhol Beag. I felt close to them. They too had loved Ian. There were so much estate matters to be sorted. I had to sort out everything for the solicitors in London.

"It was growing dark. I had just lit the candles when there was a knock on the door and before I could answer it, Hetty came flying into the room.

"'Oh my Lady, something terrible is going to happen. Don't you hear them?'

"We moved to the window. From across the loch nearly to the shore were dozens of boats, the people in them waving pitch torches and yelling.

"As they approached we suddenly realised what they were. They were going to burn or drown the Italian witch. Standing up in the first boat was Fiona.

"She was like a madwoman standing there in the glow of the torch she was carrying.

"'You killed him, you brought misery to us! You are going to pay!'

"I heard the voice of Dhol Beag. He had run down to the shore to try to pacify them.

"'So it's you, Monroe, that's at the bottom of this!' I heard him shout. 'Are you going to do what your grandfather did? Murder innocent people?'

"Dhol Mhor caught my arm. 'He won't be able to hold them off for long. Monroe has probably got all the villagers drunk and with Fiona leading them on there will be no stopping them. You have got to leave, my Lady. I will bring the pony and trap to the back. We can't risk going round the loch. They would catch us. Our only bet is to head for the garrison town and from there you could get a coach to Glasgow. If you stay away for a while things might quieten.'

"I was so afraid. Young Hetty, bless her, showed so much courage that night. She opened the curtains in my room overlooking the loch, lit dozens of candles and stood at the window in full view of the mob. 'It's her!' they yelled. 'The witch is at the window!'

"Before they realised the mistake I was well away, Dhol Mhor driving the pony and trap like a madman.

"Poor Dhol Mhor. We said goodbye in the garrison town. I hugged and kissed him. We both knew that it was goodbye.

"Later I learned through Young & Dobie, my solicitors, that Monroe tried to get the estate. If I had died he would have stood a good chance.

"When the villagers started to see sense and realised what Monroe had been up to, they turned on him and chased him from the village. And the two Donalds soon got someone to open another shop and inn.

"As you know, I never returned to Baldune.

"I travelled from country to country over many years, seeking peace in my mind.

"And now for the first time within all these years I feel, with the help of you, my darling Tansy, that I have found it.

"We must now face Ralph if we are going to save the Howard estate and help all the people there."

CHAPTER 28

TANSY looked at Gran-Mere. With the strain of re-living her story, and as Dr Brown suspected, the pain she was in, she could in no way take on Ralph.

Dr Brown thought the same thing.

"Leave it for a few days Gran-Mere. Don't worry about Ralph getting to Tansy. I will arrange for someone to watch over her for the next few days."

A few days later Gran-Mere asked Dr Brown to ask Tom and his mum and dad to come to see her.

"And you too, doctor. I would like you to hear what I have to tell."

Tansy was puzzled. Surely Gran-Mere's story had finished.

She went out to milk the goats.

Ian was strolling down the road. He waved to her.

Later, when she went to the kitchen window, there was Ian sitting on a wall nearby.

Then it dawned on her. Dr Brown had sent Ian to watch out for anyone suspicious near the cottage.

She felt so grateful to him, dear Ian. What a good friend he was.

A few days later Dr Brown, Mr and Mrs Bruce, Tom and Tansy sat round the table waiting to hear what Gran-Mere had to say and why she had called them all together.

Gran-Mere started to talk.

'Oh no,' Tansy thought. 'I don't want to hear any more of Gran-Mere's story. It's all too sad.'

Gran-Mere smiled at her once again. She amazed Tansy, reading her thoughts. "No, Tansy, this time it's a happy story." Gran-Mere turned to Tom. "Do you remember when you were a young boy and your father and mother were ill? Your father had been shot and your mother had picked up a germ from the stream."

Tom's mother and father were nodding.

"Of course we remember, and Tansy ran to fetch you."

Tom smiled at Tansy. "I was so angry with you, Tansy. I didn't want you to see how poor we were."

"Well, never mind that," Gran-Mere said. She turned to Tom's mother. "You walked from your bedroom. You were so ill. You looked at me and there was such dignity about you in such awful circumstances. I looked at you over the days I visited you and I felt more and more that I should know you. Then you came to the house a few times and when you told me about your late mother, I *knew*.

"Will you tell us your story, Jessie?"

Tom looked at Gran-Mere as if she had lost her mind.

Jessie blushed to the roots of her red hair, so like Tom's. "There isn't a lot to tell," she said. "My mother spoke very little about her past. Before she died she did speak about a little village in Scotland. I think her family had disowned her but she was very happy with my father. She was very young when I was born."

Dr Brown was nodding his head. "It fits, yes, it fits."

"Jessie. Is that the name your mother gave you?"

"No. When I was little I was called Jessica, my mother's name. And later when I played with other children they called me Jessie—and it stuck."

Tansy listened open mouthed. She knew what was coming next.

Gran-Mere smiled at Tom. "The firm you work in, Young & Dobie, as you know, are my solicitors. They have kept me in touch with Dhol Mhor and the estate. And the dates they got from Dhol Mhor and the stories you told me, Jessie, all added up. And especially when you told me your mother was a Scottish lady. She was Jessica Moncrieff before she married your father.

"Jessie, you are my late husband's cousin and as such *you* are the only heir to the Baldune estate.

"And thank God! Through you, Tom, the Moncrieff blood will carry on. My beloved Ian would be so happy."

"But what about you, Gran-Mere? Surely the estate is yours?" Tansy said.

"No, it is right that the Moncrieff blood should carry on. If I had had a child it would have been different.

"And wasn't it strange, Jessie, that when your uncle visited Sir Edward, he never thought that one day his flesh and blood would be living in Redburn?

"It took some weeks to get all the legal papers signed. Tom was going ahead of his parents to visit Baldune."

Gran-Mere was brimming over with happiness at the way things had worked out.

"And to think," Tansy said to her, "it was because you saw Jessie so like Ian. And then, Gran-Mere, that strange thing in you told you the rest."

There was so much happiness in them all that night.

Little did they know the awful thing that was yet to come to Redburn.

Ian came in the next day to visit Gran-Mere. Tansy gave him a quick hug. "Thank you, Ian, for protecting me, but you must be exhausted."

"Well, Tansy, you all had a late night, but from all the talk in the village you had an exciting one."

"Oh yes. The villagers are so excited about the Bruces' good fortune, as though it had happened to themselves."

"But what about it, Tansy? It's like a fairy tale. Imagine old Tom, our good friend, being Sir Thomas Moncrieff!"

They both went in to see Gran-Mere. She was lying back on the pillows. She didn't open her eyes when they went in. Ian went over to her. He felt her pulse. It was very faint. He turned to Tansy. "Go quickly, Tansy, get Dr Brown. I will stay with her."

Tansy raced down the road. She met Dr Brown coming from a neighbour's house. Ian was waiting for them, white faced. "I think she has gone. She never came to. She just gave a little sigh and was gone. I have never seen anything so peaceful."

Dr Brown bent over her and confirmed what Ian had said. He crossed her arms over her chest.

Tansy, too shocked to cry, looked down at her dear Gran-Mere. It was like looking at Gran-Mere the way she would have looked as a young girl. She looked so peaceful and Tansy could have sworn there was a faint smile on her face.

Aloud, Tansy said: "She has gone to her beloved Ian."

Dr Brown agreed. "Yes, last night she was so happy. She felt that she had righted a wrong she had done to Ian all those years ago. We will miss her, Tansy. She was such a big part of our lives. I think she had been in pain since the night she was attacked. Just sheer courage kept her going. She was determined to finish her story."

The whole village mourned her passing. She had helped so many of them.

CHAPTER 29

GRAN-MERE was laid to rest in the little dell in the woods—the little spot where she would sit with Tansy among the primroses and violets, teaching her all the knowledge of herbs.

Dr Brown insisted that Tansy should come to stay at his house.

"You can't be left alone and you would be company for your friend Jessie Campbell. Remember, Tansy, we will have to decide when to get things sorted out at Trent and I think there should be no more secrets about who you are. I will have a word with Sir Edward and if Ralph causes trouble he will have the power to deal with him."

Tansy kept busy, packing everything away at the cottage.

Tom came to see her. He put his arms round her. She rested her head on his shoulders for just a moment. They were suddenly shy of each other.

Sir Edward came to see Dr Brown. Tansy thought he looked worried. She went to go, to leave them to talk. He called her back.

"I think you should hear this, Tansy," he said. "Lady Frail has just come back from London. Some terrible disease is happening there."

"What do you mean, disease?" Dr Brown demanded.

Young Ian came in. "What's happening father? The house is full to bursting with all your and mother's friends."

Sir Edward looked guilty. "It's not me or your mother who invited them. Some of them we hardly know. They are all trying to escape from the disease in London."

"What of the poor people?" Tansy asked. "Where do they go?"

She was remembering the day Gran-Mere had taken her to see where the poor people lived in London. How horrified she had been.

"What are the symptoms of this disease?" Dr Brown asked. "London is always having some disease or another. It will pass." But he was worried. Redburn was only about thirty miles from London.

The stories kept coming to Redburn, each one more horrific than the last. The first victims were found in the poorer areas and some houses had as many as ten in one room, so that if one took ill, all ten would become ill.

Strangers kept arriving in Redburn. The village inn was full to overflowing. Tansy was afraid to go near the wood. Dozens of people were living there under makeshift shelters. They were the poor people from London.

Their campfires were all over the wood. Tom's father had given up trying to keep order there.

Sir Edward's bailiffs had also given up policing the woods looking for poachers. All the people there were just trying to stay alive.

Tansy called into the cottage to collect some of Gran-Mere's jars of ointments. She tried to turn the key in the lock but something seemed to be blocking it. She tried to push it.

How strange, she thought. Maybe the wind had jammed it.

She gave it a hefty push. She nearly jumped out of her skin when a voice shouted from inside.

"Get away, get away from the door! I have a gun. I will shoot!"

Tansy froze; then she got angry.

"This is my cottage! What are you doing in it? You let me in. If you don't I will go and get help from the village men. They will soon throw you out."

Something was pulled back and the door opened slowly.

A tall pale-faced man was staring at her. He had a length of wood in his hand ready to hit out at anyone coming through the door. There was no gun.

When Tansy entered he looked surprised.

"I'm sorry," he said. "I thought it was some of the ones from the woods."

A small fair-haired woman stood behind him. Then one by one children appeared. Tansy saw a look of terror on their faces.

"I haven't come to harm you. Can I sit down?" She pulled out a chair. "Now, then, tell me what this is all about." The children, Tansy guessed, were aged between seven and eleven. The eldest, a girl, looked like her mother. The two youngest, a boy and girl, were dark haired—taking after their father, she presumed.

They all sat at the kitchen table. Tansy thought the last time she had sat at this table was with Gran-Mere. What would she have made of all this?

The father started to speak. "We are so sorry, breaking into your home, but I have to protect my family. We managed to leave London just in time. The Lord Mayor closed the gates and everyone was supposed to have a certificate to leave the city. But these certificates get more and more expensive and only the rich could afford to leave. I am Bob White. This is my wife Nancy, and this is my family." He put his hand on the eldest child's shoulder. "This is my daughter Frances. I don't think we would have got out of London if it wasn't for her. She managed to trick the guards, putting on a posh voice and the guards thought we were important people and let us pass. She is a proper mimic. She can put on any voice. The two little ones—Jack here is nine…"

"And I am seven," the little girl piped up. "And my name is Mary." Little Mary made everyone smile.

"Tell me about what's happening in London. It must be something awful when so many people are running from it, giving up their homes."

Bob White looked at Tansy. "I hope to God you never see what we have seen. The children are young, they can forget, but my wife and I will never forget the horror.

"It started near the street where we lived. I am a carpenter and Nancy had a little shop selling household things. We weren't rich but not as poor as some in parts of the city. They lived in terrible poverty.

"I am told," continued Bob, "that the disease had started in the Spring and the authorities had ignored it because it had started in the poorer parts of the city. And with the summer getting hotter and hotter the disease is spreading."

Tansy looked at the small family. They all looked so tired. When she asked them if they had eaten, they shook their heads.

Tansy looked in the cupboard. There was some flour and meal left in the stone jars and a few jars of preserves.

"I'm sure we can make some kind of meal," Tansy said.

"But we were too afraid to put on a fire."

"Well, you don't have to worry about that anymore. I will let the village people know that you have my permission. Tomorrow you can go into the garden. There are quite a lot of vegetables there and the trees are full of fruit. I'm sure this thing in London will pass soon."

Bob shook his head. "Later I will talk to you, Tansy. I don't think you realise just how terrible this plague is. It is getting called the Black Death."

Tansy bade them goodbye.

"I'll come in to see you all tomorrow."

When she went back to Dr Brown's and told him about the people in her cottage, he said he would pay them a visit. "But Tansy, I have a feeling that it's not going to pass without us all getting pulled in."

A man came crawling from the wood. His groans were heard right down the street. People came out of their houses to investigate. They were all too afraid to go near him. They knew he wasn't a village man. Then one of the young children, curious, approached him.

Dr Brown, coming out of one of the houses, saw what was

happening.

"Get that child away inside, and that goes for everyone! I suspect this man has the plague."

The man's cries were pitiful.

Dr Brown approached him. His face and what he could see of his body was covered in black boils that were suppurating evil smelling matter.

Even as Dr Brown looked at him he gave a cry and Dr Brown knew he had died. Blessed relief, he thought, away from all his suffering.

Dr Brown got into action quickly. He shouted to the men: "Go and fetch some buckets of lime and a tarpaulin."

When they returned, he covered the body in lime and covered it with the tarpaulin.

"Now a grave has to be dug outside the village."

When everything was done he called a meeting of all the village people.

"That man had the plague and anyone who was in contact with him is likely to get it. Nobody must go near the wood. I know you need the wood for your cooking fires but I suggest that we have a fire outside in the square that the whole village can use."

And so the terror of the plague came to Redburn.

Tansy, Ian and Dr Brown did as much as they could to keep the village safe but they, like all the learned doctors in London, couldn't cure it because they didn't know what caused it.

Someone suggested that it was cats and dogs that spread the disease and thousands of them were killed.

CHAPTER 30

WHEN someone in a house caught the plague the body was thrown into the street and the house sealed for forty days. Someone went round with a cart up and down the streets calling, "Bring out your dead!" A red cross was painted on the door.

More of the Londoners who camped out in the wood died there. Later over twenty graves were discovered.

The first villager to catch the disease was Jessie Campbell's stepfather. He had defied the order not to go to the wood. He went to get a rabbit for the pot. He had said to Jessie's mother, "Nobody is going to tell me what to do."

Tansy and Dr Brown visited him. Tansy tried all sorts of herbs. Nothing worked. Before going in they tied masks on their faces. It was as well. The stench was terrible. He died within a few days. Two weeks later Jessie's mother died.

Dr Brown was now worried about Jessie. She had been to visit her mother the week before. He knew that if anything were to happen to her it would be in two weeks. They just had to wait. There was nothing they could do.

Tansy visited the little family in her cottage. Bob White and Nancy wanted to do something to help the villagers. They were so grateful to be allowed to stay in the cottage. Tansy suggested that they should use the garden vegetables to make lots of soup for them. Supplies were getting low in the village shop because no carriers were allowed in from London.

They heard all the stories from London. Thousands had died. The London children had a little rhyme:

> *Ring a Ring of Roses*
> *A Pocket full of Posies*
> *Attischoo Attischoo*
> *We all fall down!*

The first part of the jingle was about the red circles on the skin that developed into boils. The second line related to the belief of the people that the plague was spread by some kind of gas that had an awful smell—and so they filled their pockets with flowers to cover the smell.

The final symptom of the plague was sneezing. The fit was followed by death—'we all fall down!'

Some of the sufferers never reached the final stages. Swift death was merciful.

Jessie Campbell, after the two weeks were up, seemed fine. She hadn't succumbed to the dreaded disease. She became one of the willing helpers along with a number of other women.

They kept the fire going when evening came, burning anything not needed in, and out of their houses.

One old man came running after them one day. They had taken away the wooden seat that he sat on in the outside toilet.

With all the sensible precautions the villagers had taken, it seemed for a while that they were winning the fight against the plague.

Tom's mother and father, following exactly the orders that Dr Brown gave them, and taking every precaution, nevertheless died within three days of each other. Their deaths took the heart out of the villagers. They hardly spoke a word to each other, thinking to themselves, who next? Will it be the man or woman I am talking to today, or will it be me?

Tansy's first thought was for Tom. Thank God he was miles away in the Scottish Highlands. His poor mother and father were looking forward to going there. Especially Jessica, who was looking forward to seeing Baidune House and the estate, her mother's old home.

Tansy's heart went out to Tom. There was no way of letting him know. Messages weren't allowed out or into the village. They were completely isolated.

Tansy visited the White family nearly every day. She enjoyed their stories of London before the plague. The street they lived in was quiet and respectable although poor. Rubbish wasn't thrown onto the street. A man came with a cart to collect it from each house. Then he took it to a dump. The human waste was poured from the pails they used and put into covered drains along each street. These drains, like tunnels were crisscrossed all over London. They were so big a man could stand up in them. They were called sewers.

Sometimes on a summer's night someone would start playing a fiddle or something in the street and everyone would be out dancing and singing.

"And I could dance too," young Mary said, climbing up on Tansy's knee.

Tansy hugged her. She would miss this family when they went home.

As Tansy walked back to Dr Brown's she could hear the weeping coming from some of the houses. So many people had lost a loved one.

She thought about the story Bob White had told about all the poor people forgetting their worries and dancing in the street.

An idea started to form in her mind. The square already had a big fire burning every night. Surely the villagers would be as safe in the air outside as in their sad little cottages. As the idea formed she spoke to Dr Brown.

"An excellent idea, Tansy. It would put the heart back into the village. We won't say anything to them and let the music draw them out. I know a few of the villagers who play something."

But it was to be some time before any of it took place.

Tansy, on her usual visit to the Whites, heard sobbing when she went to the door. She went in and found them all gathered round little Mary's bed.

"Is she ill?" she demanded. Her mother pulled back the sheet that was covering her. Her dear little body had the black boils on the top of her legs and in her armpits.

Tansy ran from the room. She couldn't bear it. Dr Brown bumped into her at the door but she ran past him. She could still hear the child's wee voice echoing in her head the first time she met them—"and I am Mary, I am seven," she had piped up, thinking her father had forgotten to introduce her.

And now she lay dying and nothing anyone could do could save her.

She died in just a few days.

Of all the deaths, Mary's hit Tansy the hardest. For days she wandered about the doctor's house trying to find an answer. Why such an innocent child should die in such a way was beyond her understanding.

Dr Brown took her in hand.

"Now Tansy, people in the village still need your help. I know that there is very little we can do but little is better than nothing. And remember, Tansy, some do survive." He spoke firmly but kindly. "Now Tansy, remember the idea you had about gathering the village people together to try to cheer them up? Well, I have spoken to two men who have missed their music because they can't play in their houses while the village is in mourning. They will go to the square tonight and start playing by the fire. We will see what happens."

And so as dusk was falling the people in the village were amazed to hear the music coming from the square.

One by one the cottage doors opened and in a slow trickle to begin with, people made their way to the square. Then more and more joined them till the whole square was crowded. Then one man started to sing. Everyone joined in, some of them singing even as the tears were rolling down their cheeks.

Sir Edward and Lady Frail arrived with all the visitors that were staying with them. They all joined in

"This is wonderful," Lady Frail said. "I think we were all needing something to cheer us and to give heart to all the poor people who have lost someone."

Ian arrived, Eva clinging to his arm. He looked pale and tired. He had worked so hard along with them trying to bring some comfort to the dying.

Someone spoke to Eva and when she turned, Ian moved over to speak to Tansy. They talked about some of the cases they had attended to that day.

"You should have a few days rest, Ian. Some of the village women have been such a help. We can manage."

Ian almost snorted. "Rest. At my home? It's impossible." He waved his hand. "They all expect to be entertained. And Eva, she is the worst of the lot. She won't give me one moment's peace. She is young and strong. She should have been helping us. I never realised how completely selfish she is."

CHAPTER 31

SOMEONE touched Tansy's arm. She looked round. It was Bob White with Nancy and the children.

"We had to come to share in the hope of the village, that things will get better and our dear Mary would have loved it."

Sir Edward came over to join them. "Tansy, will you sing for us?"

Tansy hesitated. "Are you sure, Sir Edward?"

"Yes, I'm sure. Sing something they all know."

So the fiddle players started to play 'Nut Brown Maiden' and Tansy sang, her voice soaring high over the crowds.

There was complete silence when she finished. Then a roar went up. "More, Tansy, more!" And so it went on into the night.

They all drifted back to their homes with some peace in their hearts.

Ian turned to her and gave her a big hug. "You were wonderful, Tansy. You gave us all something tonight."

Eva appeared. "Come on Ian, let's get home. Away from this rabble."

Tansy sat by the fire. She threw on more wood. It was a beautiful night. She didn't want to go inside.

"So it was you, Tansy. The voice of an angel I heard as I entered the village."

Tansy looked up. Tom was looking down at her. Dear Tom, who hadn't been far from her thoughts for such a long time.

"How did you manage to get out of London?" was the first thing she could think of saying.

"Oh, I managed." There was a trace of bitterness in his voice. "I am a rich man now. It was easy to bribe."

"Oh Tom, your mother and father…"

"Yes Tansy, I know. My solicitors, Young and Dobie, managed to get a word to Baldune just a short time ago. Do you know that Londoners weren't even allowed to send letters in case they carried this dreaded plague? Oh Tansy, you should see London. It's just a nightmare. Especially in the poorer districts. People are locked up in their own houses if the plague has been there.

"There are some women who call themselves nurses, who are allowed in with some food. They get past the guard at the door and steal everything they can lay their hands on.

"The rubbish is piling up on the streets and there are dozens of rats running around."

He sat down by the fire and put his head in his hands.

"Oh Tansy, I should have been here to help poor mother and father. Did they suffer much?"

Tansy tried to comfort him. He hadn't had the time the villagers had to mourn them.

They sat by the fire, arms round each other, Tom drawing comfort from Tansy.

After a while Tansy took his hand. She felt so much older than him.

"You must come with me to stay at the doctor's."

He looked inquiringly at her. "Won't Gran-Mere mind?" So once again he had to hear bad news.

"You are a wonderful person, Tansy. Everyone's helper."

The people getting infected got less and less and it seemed as if the village was clear of the plague, but the strict routine they had carried out remained.

Tansy thought a lot about the people that had taken refuge in the Redburn woods. They saw smoke from their fires but that was all.

Dr Brown called a meeting. "The people in the woods are human beings. They have been there from the start of the plague. Talk is that twenty have died but they have not bothered the village. Certainly there is plenty of food there for them.

"I would like some volunteers to go there with me. We would of course have to take all sorts of precautions. We will cover ourselves with masks and gloves and some old clothes. We will leave a change of clothes at the edge of the woods and throw away the old ones so that we won't bring the plague back to the village."

"You have it well sorted out, doctor. I will willingly go with you," said Tom. "And me," Tansy put her hand up. "I would like to go."

Bob White volunteered.

"And me," Ian said, just coming in. Two or three of the men from the village wanted to come. Jessie Campbell joined them. In all there would be ten of them.

When they entered the wood they were all a bit nervous. They moved carefully and they were a good distance in before they came on an encampment. A tall man met them.

"I am Soldier. Well," he smiled, "that's the name I got because of my years in the army."

Dr Brown and his supporters looked round. It was quite unbelievable. It looked like a proper village. There were rows of shelters all in neat rows round a clearance in the centre. They were made of intertwined hazel branches, the roofs mainly moss and ferns and all sorts of bits from the woods.

Dr Brown, still amazed, said, "But you are all Londoners! Where did you manage to get the ideas?"

"Well," Soldier said. "I am not a Londoner. I was brought up not far from here. My father was a charcoal burner. You could say the woods were my life until both my parents died and that's when I joined the army. When I left it was with the rank of sergeant. I'm used to giving orders and getting them obeyed. When I ran from London it was my instinct that took me to the wood. I think it was the same for all these people, but if I hadn't been here they would surely have perished. We lost twenty to the plague." He pointed to a large cairn of stones. "They are all buried there. I managed to get most of their names before they died, so when this is all over I can let any remaining relatives know where they are buried. Londoners are quick to learn and in no time they were setting snares for rabbits." He looked guilty for a moment. "I'm afraid I had to steal a few things from outlying farms. Some things to cook in, for instance. When I was in the army I served abroad for a number of years. It's great what can be learned on survival courses, so it stood me in good stead here and all these people look on me as their leader. Do you know that the cause of the plague has been found to be rats?"

"How do you know this?" Dr Brown demanded. "It was thought that it was cats and dogs—and now they say rats?"

Soldier looked ill at ease. "I know, because I was in London only last week." He was whispering. "I don't want any of them to know I went there."

Tansy was cross. "How *could* you? You could have brought the disease back."

Soldier answered her: "I done what you people, I presume, have done to take precautions," he continued. "Don't you realise that all the people in the wood had to find out things? We are in isolation here. The plague could have been over for months without us knowing. This way when it is over I can let them know."

"How did they come to the conclusion that it was rats?" Tom asked.

"Well, apparently the disease has been going on for some time in Holland. Not as bad as the London one. Anyway, I think it was them that discovered that it was black rats that carried the plague, from fleas that they carried. The rats came to London on a Dutch ship. They multiplied quickly among the filth and dirt in the poorer areas of

London.

"Don't ask me how I know all this, but if you look at your boundary board it will tell you all this. It will also tell you that there had been no more deaths in London for three weeks. Thanks be to God, I think it is over."

Rejoicing went on all over England. A few isolated cases still occurred in some of the villages. One of the villages was Trent. Tansy was busy hanging Rue over doors and getting the villagers to help. Each room held a jar of the plant because she remembered Gran-Mere saying that rats hated Rue. What a pity, she thought, that they had not known earlier that it was rats that carried the plague. Maybe this simple herb could have saved lives.

Tansy was so happy to have Tom home, even though she knew it would be for a short time. He would have to go back to his new home in Scotland.

They were all sitting round Dr Brown's table discussing everything that had happened in the past year.

"I will have to go to Trent," Tansy said. "I feel that I have to help the people there."

"I will go with you Tansy," Tom volunteered. "I think we will all go. We are not needed here just now."

"Can I go?" Jessie Campbell asked.

"Of course, Jessie. You aren't needed in the house just now." Dr Brown suggested that they should go there, prepared as if they were going to the woods.

Tom and Tansy were left alone as everyone went off to prepare for their visit to Trent.

"Are you happy in your Highland village, Tom?" Tansy asked.

"Oh yes, I have never been happier, Tansy. It is so different. As soon as the city of Glasgow is left behind, it's like a different world. The tall mountains that seem to change every day. The little streams flowing into the sea, as clear as crystal. I would love you to see it, Tansy. Isn't it strange, Tansy, that we both should have inherited an estate?

"Mine is small in comparison with the Howard estate. I do hope that you will be happy there, Tansy. We both have such a big responsibility."

Tansy felt a coldness clutch at her heart. There was no doubt about Tom meaning, the estates were going to keep them apart.

News came to them from Soldier that the people in the wood were preparing to go back to London, but they wanted to invite all of Redburn to a party in the wood as a thank you for allowing them to stay. In other villages the Londoners were chased out by the people, so afraid of them carrying the plague.

Mr and Mrs White asked Tansy if they could stay a bit longer in the cottage. They decided that they preferred the country to the town and if Bob could find plenty of work as a carpenter they would make Redburn their permanent home.

The Londoners in the wood must have been there for nearly a year. They were now desperate to go back to their homes, though at the same time worried about what they would find there. Sir Edward and Lady Frail went to the party.

Sir Edward made a speech telling them that the shelters they had made would be left so that if any of them found themselves homeless, they could come back. Soldier thanked him and said that he would like to come back occasionally to the wood. He had found such peace there.

Ian drew Tansy aside. "I'm leaving tomorrow, Tansy. I have enjoyed helping Dr Brown and I have learned such a lot from him. I'm going to Glasgow to start my studies. They seem to be so far advanced in medicine."

"I'm going to miss you so much, Ian. You are such a good friend. I am sorry that I won't have your support when I go to Trent."

"You will be fine, Tansy. Dr Brown and Tom will be with you when you come face to face with Ralph."

Tansy put her arms round him and gave him a big hug. She looked over his shoulder and saw Tom watching them. He had such an unhappy look on his face. Tansy wondered what he was thinking.

CHAPTER 32

THE next day Tansy, Dr Brown and Tom set off for Trent. The first stop was at the inn in Trent village.

Dr Brown wanted to find out just what was happening there, and how many people had the plague.

A few of the locals gathered round and explained where the sick were. They had had a few deaths in the past few weeks but there had been a lot more on the estate itself. It had been a bad time. The people in the estate houses had a bad time even before the plague hit them, Ralph refusing to pay wages to the workers for being five minutes late for work. And at the end of each month when they went to the big house to get their wages, Ralph would say he had no money. And one month when the men argued with him he threatened them with a gun.

All the men had families. They could do nothing, for Ralph owned the houses they lived in. They would have starved if it weren't for the help they got from the neighbouring farm, the Gordons.

The Gordons father and daughter never set foot on Howard ground after an argument many years ago.

"I know about that quarrel," Tansy said.

"Oh," one of the locals said, "now how would you know about that? You are just a slip of a girl."

Dr Brown knocked on the table for silence. He pulled Tansy up beside him. "Now everybody let me introduce Miss Tansy Howard, or Lady Tansy. She is the daughter of the late Kathryn and Michael Howard. She is the rightful owner of the Howard estate." He went on to explain to the open-mouthed villagers all the details. Everyone went quiet; then a great cheer went up and they all wanted to shake Tansy's hand. The news spread through the village like wildfire.

Tansy spoke to them about her life with Gran-Mere and the happiness she had had living at Redburn.

"But you are not going back to live there," one of the men asked.

Tansy hadn't thought so far ahead. Where *would* she live? Ralph still had the estate.

Dr Brown came to the rescue.

"Now, one thing at a time. First of all, we are here to help the sick. We will stay here at the inn and then Lady Tansy will want to get to know the estate and especially all the people who work on it."

Tansy was horrified at the state of the cottages the workers lived in. It was obvious that they were getting left to fall to bits and in Ralph's madness if any of the workers tried to do repairs themselves they were sacked, left without work or somewhere to live. Many of them had taken to the road and become beggars.

Dr Brown couldn't understand why Ralph, so desperate to keep the estate, should let it become so run down.

A lot of his so-called friends from London had been given some of the cottages but they refused to do any work on the estate and Ralph had thrown them out.

Dr Brown remembered the way things used to be. Cottages and everything else on the estate were kept in such good order that people would come for miles to admire the estate and get ideas.

It took nearly a week to go round the estate. Tansy was amazed at how big it was. One day at breakfast in the inn she turned to Tom and Dr Brown. "I think it is now time for me to face up to Ralph. I have been putting it off long enough."

"I agree," Tom said. "We were just waiting for you to decide."

The driveway to the house seemed endless before the house came into view.

Tansy gasped. She wasn't prepared for the size of it, a huge majestic building. The turret at each gable gave it the look of a very large castle.

She heard Tom draw in his breath.

"Well, that's some building! Let's go and see the wicked ogre that lives there."

As they got closer to the house they could see the terrible neglect. The paint was peeling and some of the windows were broken with the curtains hanging from them.

No smoke was coming from the chimneys, so either there was no one in the house or, if there were, they would be very cold in such a huge house.

As they approached, the front door swung open. A man stood there. He said nothing, just staring at them.

Tansy knew that this was the man who had wanted her dead. She saw someone who might at one time have been almost handsome but now just a wreck of a man. He kept staring at Tansy. He was barefoot with only a thin robe covering him.

Then he spoke directly to her. "So you have come to avenge your father's death and to take all this away from me! You've arrived too soon. In a few weeks there would have been nothing left. The cottages and this heap of Howard stone would be raised to the ground. I have been ill, hence the delay of my plans."

Tansy took a step towards him.

"You wicked, wicked man! You sent those men to harm Gran-Mere and you hated my father. You wanted this estate so badly I think you must have sold your soul to the Devil."

Before Tom and Dr Brown could move he grabbed hold of Tansy.

He pressed her against his chest. Because she was small she only came up to his armpits. The stench that came from him reminded her of the awful smell of the plague.

She struggled to get away but he kept pressing her closer. Tom grabbed hold of him and gave him a hefty punch. The man let Tansy go. His robe opened. They all recoiled in horror. His body, round his armpits and across his stomach, was covered in suppurating boils. He had the plague.

He laughed a devilish laugh. "And now you, Michael's daughter, I am leaving you a parting gift of the plague!"

Tom and Dr Brown half carried Tansy away. They saw Ralph sliding down the side of the door. They didn't go back. They knew that in a day or maybe in just a few hours he would be dead.

Tom tried to comfort Tansy. All she could think of was to get away, back to Redburn and to Dr Brown's house where she felt safe.

She knew that the next two or three weeks would be the longest of her life. She felt convinced she would die.

Ralph had pressed her close to his suppurating body and she knew that it took less than that to get the plague.

"Before we go back I would like to go to the church to see where my mother and father were laid to rest, but I would like to go there alone."

"Of course, Tansy. If that's what you want." Tom was a bit dubious. "Do be careful, Tansy. There are still a lot of desperate people around."

Tansy stood in the doorway of the church looking in. It felt so strange. Her mother and father had walked down that aisle to be married, so happy and so much in love. They had such a short time together before they went down the same aisle to lie together in death.

Tansy didn't realise she was sobbing out loud until she felt a gentle touch on her shoulder and a woman's voice spoke. "I know this must be very hard for you, but, my dear, they are at peace."

Tansy looked round. The woman had such a kind face. Tansy felt she had known her all her life. The woman put her arms out and held Tansy close. "Tansy, my dear child, you are so like your mother. I got a shock when I first saw you. I am Katy, your mother's best friend. I have been longing to meet you all these years, but it was never safe. Ralph had so many spies around."

Tansy couldn't believe it. She felt so happy. Here was a woman who could tell her all the precious things about her mother—all the little things that mattered so much to her. Gran-Mere had done her best but she was of a different generation.

It was Katy who told her, standing there in the church, that Ralph was found dead that morning. He had died all alone.

Tansy felt some pity for him He had everything, yet wanted more.

"I have got to go now. Tom and Dr Brown are waiting for me at the inn." Then she remembered. She could have caught the plague from Ralph and she could have given it to Katy when she hugged her.

"Oh God, how awful. When will it ever end?"

"Now Tansy, don't start thinking like that. Off you go now and I will meet you here in two or three weeks."

They were only back a few days when news came of a terrible fire of London. Hundred of homes had been destroyed, mostly among the poorer parts. Soldier was one of the unfortunates. He came back to the wood in Redburn. Soon more of the homeless made their way back, glad to have some shelter.

Tansy tried to keep occupied, terrified of the fate she thought was in store for her. Every day she examined herself, looking for the telltale signs of the plague.

She thought a lot about Trent and the estate. How was she going to manage it? There was so much to be done. The big house itself would need months of work done to it. Ralph, half mad as he was, was still an authority to be obeyed, whereas she was only a very young person brought up in a little cottage.

She was very close to the third week of her isolation and there were still no symptoms of the plague.

She had survived.

CHAPTER 33

SHE went to look for Tom to share her joy with him. She ran to the door. Tom was walking with Eva. She couldn't have gone back to London with the others.

As she watched she saw her putting her arm around Tom's waist, lifting her face for Tom to kiss her.

She dashed into the house. She couldn't breathe. 'I've lost him,' kept going through her head.

She made her way to her bedroom, then the tears came—hot sobbing tears that hurt her chest.

Jessie was knocking on the door.

"Are you in, Tansy? Are you going to walk to the village with me?"

"I'll be out in a minute, Jessie. Just give me time to freshen up."

She washed away the tearstains, brushed her hair, threw back her shoulders and spoke to herself in the mirror. "You are a Howard. You have the good blood of generations in your veins. Now get out there and don't let anyone see how you are hurting."

It was wonderful to be out after being confined to the house for nearly three weeks.

They heard more stories about the fire in London. Over five hundred homes that had been destroyed would take years to replace because they weren't going to be built with wood, but with stone, so that there would never be such a terrible fire there again.

Tansy and Jessie on their way home met Tom. He was on his own.

"I was looking for you, Tansy. I will have to leave on the afternoon coach. I should have left weeks ago but I had to wait to make sure you were all right."

Tansy heard herself saying coolly, "You shouldn't have bothered about me Tom, I had all my friends round me."

Tom looked at her, a hurt puzzled look on his face. Even Jessie looked surprised.

"Why all the hurry?" Jessie asked him. "Are you going back to Scotland?"

"Well, yes, I am, but first I must go to London. Because of the fire the office of Young & Dobie was in a mess with the files, and even though I no longer work there I feel obliged to help out."

He turned to Tansy. "I'll miss you, Tansy. Maybe the next time I come to Redburn it will be to visit you at your estate."

"Well, with the mess it's all in, that will be a long time." She held out her hand to him. "Thanks, Tom, for all your help. I hope the next time you visit it won't be on such a sad occasion. You must miss your mother and father. I'm sure when you visit again Dr Brown will let you stay with him. Come now Jessie, we must hurry back. Dr Brown will be home for tea soon."

With that she took Jessie's arm and marched off, leaving Tom standing looking after them.

As soon as they were out of earshot Jessie turned on Tansy.

"Just what has got into you? Why were you so nasty to Tom? Couldn't you see how hurt he was at your coldness?"

Tansy marched on. "I don't know what you are talking about, Jessie. And anyway it's none of your business."

Later that night when Jessie passed Tansy's door she heard her crying and she wondered what Tom had done to upset her.

She remembered seeing Eva at the house earlier in the day. Now, she thought to herself, I wonder if that bitch had anything to do with it?

The next day Tansy made her way to Trent. She remembered that she had arranged to meet Katy at the church if everything had gone well with her showing no signs of the black plague.

Katy was there. She gave Tansy a big hug. "Thank God," she said. "I lost your mother, my best friend. I didn't want to lose her daughter as well. Come on Tansy, let's ride to my home. We can have lunch. My father is looking forward to meeting you."

Tansy looked around as they rode. The Gordon estate, although much smaller than the Howard one, was in immaculate condition. Not a wall or fence needed repair and when they arrived at the house it was the same. It was a good solid two-storey building. Inside, the same idea—the furniture dark oak. The room would have been dark and drab if it wasn't for the beautiful china displayed on a huge dresser. And on the table a vase of early daffodils.

The door opened. An old man came in. He shuffled into the room, his back bent over. He looked at Tansy and gave her such a lovely smile that Tansy saw that this was not such an old man.

"Now Katy, why take this lovely young lady into the parlour? What's wrong with a nice warm kitchen?"

Katy turned to Tansy. "This is my father. He never stops bossing me around."

Tansy could see such a lot of affection there was between them. She felt a sadness for a moment. Would she have been like this with her father?

They did end up in the kitchen sitting around the table after a huge lunch. Katy and father spoke a lot about the Howard estate and about what it had been like before Ralph.

"I can't do much work nowadays but I can help you with advice when you come to take over," he smiled at her. "Lady Tansy."

"Oh please," she said. "Just Tansy. I feel so uncomfortable being called Lady."

"Well, my dear, you will have to get used to it. The village people have always had someone to look up to on the estate, apart from

Ralph. That's the way it's been for a few hundred years." Again he smiled. "But to Katy and I you will be Tansy."

Tansy reached up and gave him a hug. He was such a dear kind man. Tansy could see he was in a lot of pain

"You and your father are very close, Katy."

"Yes, I suppose we are. We have both worked hard here, but as you saw, father is suffering from all the hard work. But then again it's something he has loved doing."

"You never married, Katy?" Tansy asked.

Katy smiled. "I just never seemed to have the time, and the years have gone so quickly."

Tansy looked at her. She thought she was a very attractive woman.

"Well, you could still meet someone."

"Oh Tansy, you are so like your mother. She always tried to push me into doing things. I was such a stick-in-the-mud. Quite happy going about the farm in old clothes. Your mother would have me going with her on shopping trips. We had such fun. I still miss her so much. Now Tansy, let's start talking about you. What is going to happen to the Howard estate? There is such a lot to do there now. I am willing to lend a hand to help with livestock and things like that. Why don't you come to live here for a few weeks? You can see how things are done and we can sit and decide on the things to do first on your estate."

Tansy felt a great sense of relief at Katy's offer. She did have great friends. But no one, including herself, had any idea of running an estate.

Dr Brown was sad to see her leave but realised it was an excellent idea.

So Tansy moved in with Katy and her father. During the day they were out attending to the livestock. Tansy, wearing a pair of borrowed Wellingtons from Katy, loved every minute of it. It was all so new and wonderful. At night they sat at the kitchen table deciding the best way of going about the rescue of the Howard estate.

"It's going to cost an awful lot of money," Katy said. "How are thing with you financially, Tansy?"

134

"Do you know, I really have no idea. Dr Brown may know."

"Well, my advice, Tansy, is to visit this solicitor of Gran-Mere's. I will go with you. Do you know the address?"

Tansy was silent. Of course she knew the address. If they went there maybe Tom would still be there. Her heart started to hammer at the thought.

"Are you all right, Tansy?"

"Yes, I am fine. It is very good of you, Katy, and maybe Dr Brown would come with us."

The next week Tansy, Dr Brown and Katy set off for London.

Tansy remembered the last time going to London with Gran-Mere. The coach trip seemed to go on forever. Such a lot had happened since then.

They weren't prepared for the utter devastation as they approached the centre of the city. The coach passed through the area of slums that Gran-Mere had taken her to. The whole street had been burnt to the ground.

The government had thrown up makeshift shelters. What the plague and fire had done could not have been worse than the way those poor people had to live. Dr Brown said that as many died of cold and hunger.

Katy was so angry. "Poor people. I wouldn't treat an animal on the farm like this."

The coach dropped them off near the solicitors.

"Let's get the business over first; then we could maybe go for a meal."

"I don't think I will be able to eat anything after seeing these poor people," Tansy said.

"I'm sorry the coach took that route in." Dr Brown patted her shoulder. "You are young and young people have good appetites. Yours will come back, I'm sure."

They approached Young & Dobbie Solicitors. Some of the houses round about had been burnt but nothing in comparison with the poorer areas.

They were shown into a very comfortable lounge by a receptionist. She said that one of the partners would be with them shortly. Tansy's heart was thumping. Would Tom come to see them if he knew they were there?

A man came into the room carrying a bundle of papers. He was short and stout with a happy smiling face. He had glasses perched on the tip of his nose.

As he walked towards them he proceeded to drop one paper after another. Dr Brown went to help him pick them up.

"Thank you Sir. So clumsy of me." He held out his hand. "I'm Mr Young." He shook hands with them all.

"And you are Tansy. I am so very happy to meet you at last. Your Gran-Mere was a dear friend of mine and my partner, Mr Dobbie. Now, if you make yourselves comfortable I will go through all this paperwork with you. You understand it goes back a number of years."

He turned to Tansy. "You will be aware that your late mother Kathryn Howard left Dr Brown as executor of her estate or rather the estate that your grandparents left. Unfortunately things did not work out for your grandparents and with the result not a lot of money was left for you, Tansy." He shuffled the papers around. "There is only a cash amount of £5,000. A number of pieces of jewellery that we have had valued for you should raise another £5,000."

"I expected it to be around that amount," Dr Brown said. "I hope you are not too disappointed, Tansy."

"Well, the thing is, doctor, I never really gave it much thought, but now I realise that I am going to need a great deal of money for the repairs on the Howard estate."

Mr Young was looking quite uncomfortable. "Now, as you know, Gran-Mere had quite a substantial amount of money from the Baldune estate in Scotland. Initially it was all to go to you, Tansy, but then as you know a new heir was found."

CHAPTER 34

"**GRAN-MERE** believed that you would be very well off as the heir to the Howard estate. She transferred all the proceeds that she had received from Baldune to the new owner."

There was silence as he finished speaking. Tansy's first thought was how strange that it should have been Tom who was going to deprive her of the money she desperately needed if the Howard estate was to survive. Poor Gran-Mere, always doing what she thought was right.

The silence continued when they left the solicitors. "I'm sure Tom would help you," Dr Brown suggested.

Tansy turned to him. "Please don't even suggest such a thing. I don't ever want Tom to know anything about it. Please understand, doctor."

Katy turned to Tansy. "Don't worry, my dear. Between us we will get something sorted out for the estate. And £10,000 is still quite a lot of money. You will be able to get a lot of work done for that."

Tansy cheered up at her words. "Yes, you are right. Now I can't wait to get started on the plans."

Once again Tansy and Katy were sitting at the kitchen table. This time they knew exactly how much money there was to spend.

Tansy had been thinking about it all day. She was remembering the poor people in London, old shacks for homes. It could happen here on what had been the most prosperous estate within hundreds of miles. Already the workers' houses were in need of repair. Some of the roofs were leaking so badly that even their beds were getting soaked when it rained.

She spoke to Katy. "I think that I would like to start repairing the workers' cottages. I noticed that there are several of them so badly in need of repair that they are lying empty."

"That would be the ones that Ralph's friends lived in," Katy told her.

"Well, why don't I start repairing them, and when each one is done the workers from the other cottages can move in till eventually all the cottages are back to the way they used to be."

"That's a wonderful idea, Tansy, but where are you going to get the workers to do all that?"

"I don't know, but it will be a start. I think I will go to the village tomorrow and get one or two to start dumping all the rubbish inside them. I'm sure they would be grateful getting a few shillings doing this."

She had not ventured near the big house since her encounter with Ralph. It can wait, she thought. But all the steadings, the barn, the stables would have to be repaired quickly. It was going to be a mammoth task but, she thought, 'I'll do it and show Tom and that Eva. But most of all I'll do it for mother and dear father who had such pride in their heritage.'

On the way back to Katy's she passed the workers' cottages. A lot of activity was going on. Old furniture and rubbish was getting dumped out on the road. She stopped to thank the men doing the job so quickly till she realised that it was half a dozen women. "Good day, my Lady!" one of them shouted. "We are happy to take on any work. Just you say what. It will be good for us to have a few shilling in our pockets!" Bless them, Tansy thought. She felt so encouraged by them.

She tried to get some men from the village who would be capable of joiner work, replacing doors and windows and even some parts of the roofs, but there were none. The men who would have helped were busy at their jobs on the estate. Once again Tansy felt that she was facing a brick wall.

She decided to get away from her problems. She went to visit Jessie at Dr Brown's and catch up on all the Redburn news.

The first thing Jessie said after giving her a hug was, "You have got thin, Tansy. Is that big estate of yours giving you too much worry?"

"Never mind me, Jessie. How are things here?"

"Well, we are all happy to be alive. I think we all learned a lesson thinking that it could be one of us next to catch the plague. The people in the wood have been great. They have helped so many of us with odd jobs. They look up to Soldier as their boss. I think there are about ten of them altogether. They really have taken to country life."

"What about the White family? Are they still in the cottage?"

"Yes. I don't think they want to go back to London, and Nancy White visits young Mary's grave every day."

As Jessie spoke, an idea was forming in Tansy's mind.

She called in to see the White family. It seemed strange, going into the cottage and no Gran-Mere standing in the kitchen sorting out all the herbs.

They were so pleased to see her.

"Are you still happy living here?" Tansy asked.

"Oh yes, we love it," Bob had hesitated. "There is only one thing. There is very little work for me here."

"Now Bob," Nancy scolded him, "just be patient. Sir Edward is talking about building more cottages."

"If I asked you," Tansy said, "would you come to work for me on the Howard estate? Before you reply, let me explain. A lot of work has to be done on the workers' cottages and the steadings. It would mean you travelling back and forward every day. I would sort that out for you. When the cottages are all finished you could have one and there would be a job for you for life on the estate. There would be very little money to begin with, but once the estate is back to its full strength, things will improve." Tansy got up to leave. "I'll let you think it over."

"There is no need for us to think about it, we will do it!" They stood hand in hand.

"What about the children?" Tansy asked. "Don't they want to go back to London?"

"No, we don't," they answered together. "I am nine," Jack said. "I could help on the farm and maybe when the big house is ready I could work there."

Tansy went back to tell Katy and her father the good news.

"I'm sure things will work out fine for you, lass," Katy's father said.

Tansy gave him a hug. In the short time she had stayed with them she noticed that he had become weaker. She wondered if Katy realised just how ill her father was.

It was only a few days afterwards, when Katy went in to waken him, that she found he had passed away in his sleep.

She sobbed in Tansy's arms. "I have known for a long time that he was very ill. He tried to keep it from me. He was so glad when you came to be company for me. He was a good land man. I think he would have liked to have seen me married with children, but it wasn't to be."

His funeral took place a few days afterwards. The whole village attended. He was so well liked.

Sir Edward spoke to Tansy after the funeral. "How are you managing? You have a big undertaking getting it back to the way it was before Ralph tried to destroy it. You know it could take years?

"Now, I have a favour to ask you, Tansy. I am having a musical evening one night next week. A lot of important people are coming to stay for the weekend. They are people I need to help me renew the village, getting new houses and decent sanitation. One or two people are coming from London to entertain them, but do you think that you could sing even one song, Tansy?"

She smiled at him. "Of course I will, Sir Edward. Will Ian be there?"

"Well, this I don't know. He is in the middle of exams just now. It's quite a journey from Glasgow."

Tansy was quite excited about the invitation until she realised she didn't have anything to wear. "What am I going to do?" she wailed to Katy. "I don't want to go to London to buy one. Think of the money it would cost that could be used on one of the cottages." Katy smiled. Poor Tansy had to grow up so fast, thinking about the roof of a cottage rather than buying a pretty dress.

Later that evening Tansy was sitting at the kitchen table, as usual, trying to work out all the money needed for the repairs.

She heard a *thump, thump* on the stairs. She dashed out to see what was happening and there was Katy pulling a large trunk down the stairs. Katy was red in the face. "Well, there better be something decent in here after this effort," she said. "Now Tansy, let's see if there is anything here that you could wear to your musical evening."

The trunk seemed to be full of dresses and evening capes.

"Mother and father went to a lot of posh events, usually at the big house." Every dress was carefully folded in tissue.

"Oh," Tansy said. "Some of them are really beautiful." She picked up a dress of silver lame. "Look at the style of this one. I saw one like it in a shop window in London."

She squealed in delight when she pulled out a cape in silver lame to match.

"Why don't you go and try them on?" Katy said. "My mother was neat like you. They do smell a bit of mothballs but we have a whole week to get it sorted.

"Can you sew, Tansy? In case they need alterations. I'm afraid I'm not much good at it. I'm better with a hay fork."

Tansy was happy that she was there with her, keeping her mind occupied. She knew just how much she missed her father.

Tansy came into the room wearing the dress. "It fits well, Katy. Just a bit taken in at the waist."

Katy stared open mouthed at her.

"My God Tansy, you are really beautiful."

The dress, off the shoulder, showed off her creamy white skin—just low enough to show her cleavage.

"Do you think I could wear it, Katy? It's not too bold?"

"No, it's perfect!"

She went rummaging in the trunk again and produced a pair of silver shoes and a small evening bag.

"You have *got* to wear these, Tansy! If they are too big we will stick something under the insole. And if they are too wee we will cut a bit off for your toes."

They clung together, laughing, and when she tried them on they were just slightly big. But as Katy had said, that could be sorted.

Katy walked round and round Tansy examining every inch of the dress just to make sure there was no damage after its years of being wrapped up in tissue and placed, she was sure, lovingly in the trunk.

Now Tansy couldn't wait for the night to arrive. She put all the worries about the estate out of her mind.

Sir Edward, true to his word, sent a coach to fetch her. One of the servants was at the door. He came down and helped her from the coach and took her into the entrance hall. Another man, a footman, led the way into the large room she remembered from that fateful Halloween such a long time ago.

The footman announced her. "Lady Tansy Howard." It seemed to Tansy that there were hundreds of people in the room, all with their beautiful dresses and glittering jewellery. Tansy was glad she had held on to one or two pieces of her mother's jewellery. Tonight she wore a sapphire and diamond necklace. The brilliance of the sapphire paid tribute to her blue eyes sparkling with excitement.

When the footman announced her the chatter in the room stopped. Tansy, embarrassed, just stood there, not knowing what to do.

CHAPTER 35

SIR Edward and Lady Frail came to meet her. "Do come in, my dear. So many people want to meet you. You are looking very beautiful tonight."

As she passed a young group a voice said, "Well, she certainly knows how to make an entrance." Tansy knew that sneering voice. She carried on walking, ignoring her. So she was here—that hateful Eva.

Tansy met so many people who invited her to their homes. Everyone was so friendly that she lost her shyness, and when Sir Edward asked her if she was ready to sing she didn't hesitate. She walked to where the musicians were playing and had a quiet word with them. She had decided to sing an Italian song that Gran-Mere had taught her.

As she started to sing the room went deadly quiet. Her clear young voice rose higher and higher. It seemed to soar to the roof and beyond. When she finished the silence continued.

Tansy thought, "I shouldn't have chosen that Italian song. They didn't like it."

Then the clapping started. And the cheers. "Sing again Tansy," Sir Edward said.

"But I don't know what to sing."

"Remember the song you sang round the village fire?"

Tansy remembered. And yes, she remembered Tom arriving just as she finished singing. They were so close that night. How did things go wrong between them? But she knew it was Eva. She remembered Gran-Mere warning her the night of her sixteenth birthday when Eva had deliberately spilled wine on her dress.

"Just be careful Tansy," she had said. "It was someone like her that ruined my life."

Sir Edward was waiting and everyone was still clapping and cheering. She started to sing 'Nut Brown Maiden'. When she had finished an elderly man and his wife came up to her. Tansy was surprised to see tears in their eyes.

"My darling, you must come to our home," the lady said. "To let our friends hear your beautiful voice." She told the man to give her their card. Tansy put it in her little silver bag and forgot about it.

She made her way to the powder room. She felt quite drained with all the excitement. She picked the worst time to go there. Eva was there with some of the women. She looked up and saw Tansy coming in. She turned to the women. "Now I'm sure you all know Sir Tom Moncrieff." When one of the women nodded she said in a loud voice, "Well, Tom and I are getting engaged. It will be in the paper soon." She looked across at Tansy. "Of course you know Tom, don't you, Tansy?"

Tansy thought, 'What a vicious streak that was in her. She would find the weakest spot in someone and exploit it. She has certainly found my weak spot but I will never let her know how much it hurts me.'

"Yes, Eva, I do know Tom. We have been friends since childhood. Congratulations Eva. Tom is a very fine man." She turned and walked out of the room, sick at heart. She said her goodbyes to Sir Edward and Lady Frail. The coach was waiting to take her home. Eva had once again spoilt her night. No, she corrected her thoughts. Not her night, but her life.

Katy looked at her anxiously next morning. "Are you all right, Tansy? You look really pale and ill. Tell me all about last night. Did you enjoy yourself?"

Tansy pulled herself together. "I'm fine, Katy. I never slept well last night. I think it was all the excitement." She told Katy all that went on. "I had such a wonderful time and everyone thought my dress was beautiful. In fact, one very posh lady, full of you could tell the most expensive jewellery, asked who my dressmaker was. I managed to avoid an answer."

Tansy could tell that Katy was feeling proud that she had been part of it.

The following days Tansy put Eva out of her mind by throwing herself into the estate work. Bob White arrived and it was decided that the barn should be the first to be repaired. Tansy left him to decide what was needed.

She rode for miles round the estate with one of the old workers. Some of the livestock was in pretty poor condition. "But don't worry about that. We are going to get help from the Gordon farm," Tansy told him. "And Katy tells me that in a few months' time they will all be fine."

Katy complained that Tansy was working too hard. "You are out from dawn till dusk."

"Now Katy," Tansy said, "you are the one to talk. You are out before me most mornings."

Things were beginning to happen on the estate. The cottages had been cleared of all the rubbish and Bob had made a start on the barn.

Most of the fields were enclosed with hedges or stone walls. It would take quite a lot of time for the estate workers to repair them and of course the estate workers would have to work extra hours, which meant more money.

Dr Brown came to see her. "How are things with you Tansy? Are you managing?"

Tansy shook her head. "Well, doctor, thing are pretty desperate moneywise. It's going to take years to get the estate paying again. It's taking in barely enough to pay the workers. The ten thousand pounds won't cover even half the repairs."

"Well," Dr Brown said, "there has been a bit of help offered. No, not money," he said when Tansy made to protest.

"Soldier and some of the men in the wood have offered to help you. I will bring them out to see you tomorrow and you can talk to them."

The next day Dr Brown arrived with Soldier and one of the men. They met in the yard. Soldier looked fit and well in spite of living in the wood.

"Now," he said to Tansy, "we don't want money from you for the work, but maybe you could give us food in return?" He was looking around. "This is a grand place you have here. Now look at some of them outbuildings. They are better than some of the village cottages. Now, Lady Tansy, I have thought, would it not be a good idea if we repaired one of them? We could live in it and be here to get the work done. All we would need from you would be food and maybe firewood."

Tansy was overwhelmed. First Bob White, and now Soldier, all willing to help.

They arrived the next day, Soldier and three of the men from the wood. Some of the other men had wives and children with them in the wood and they had decided to go back to London.

The damage in the barn was not as bad as they first thought and in a few days Soldier and his men had the repairs done. They slept on the hay and Katy had arrived with blankets for them. They built a fire in the yard and they built a contraption over it to hold pots and pans. Katy arrived every day with large pans of meat and fresh bread.

There was such a happy air about the place that it caught on to the rest of the estate workers. They all had had such a bad time with Ralph that they had lost interest in their work.

The animals had been badly neglected but now the cattleman informed Tansy that some of the cattle would be ready for the next sales.

Things were going so well. The roof on the first cottage had been repaired and Bob had done a great job inside. Soldier and his men, when they had finished the barn, went to help. Tansy couldn't believe it when she went to see it. It looked like a new cottage. They had even built a new fireplace. Bob had collected a pile of wood from round about the estate and made a good solid bed with it.

"Now," he told Tansy, "I will finish off the loft and make a couple of beds up there for children."

Katy was in her element cooking for Soldier and the men, bringing down bits and pieces for the cottage.

"What about your own work?" Tansy asked her.

"Oh, there are plenty men there to do it. They are a good lot and don't worry, Tansy. I still keep a good eye on things."

Tansy chose the first family to go into the finished cottage. Theirs was the one in most need of repair. They were speechless with happiness. No more soaking wet beds to go into at night.

One cottage after another was repaired. Tansy was so busy it helped her to forget the terrible night at Sir Edward's when Eva told her she was getting engaged to Tom.

Tansy, tired out, slept well into the morning. It was the smell of bacon frying that roused her. How strange, neither she nor Katy ate breakfast.

When she went to the kitchen, there was Soldier, sleeves rolled up busy cooking at the range.

"Come on in. Tansy. I decided that you and Katy needed to have a decent breakfast. You especially, Tansy. You have been looking so pale."

Tansy was bewildered at Soldier's appearance in Katy's house.

"And where is Katy?" she asked.

"Now that I don't rightly know," he said. "I have been up since the crack of dawn. I came here to get some orders about the dairy from you. It needs a fair bit of work. As I said, I have been up since dawn. I have been drawing the big house. I wanted to give you a present of it for all your kindness." He unrolled it on the table.

Tansy was amazed. He had been absolutely meticulous with every detail.

Katy came in. "Why, hello Soldier." She too seemed surprised to see him.

Again Soldier explained why he was there. "Now Katy and Lady Tansy, are you both going to eat the lovely breakfast I have prepared?"

They both laughed. Tansy looked at Katy. There was something in her expression as she looked at Soldier that made her wonder.

Could it be possible that Katy, after all the years of being on her own, had found someone? She started thinking. Katy never missed a day of coming to the cottages, always with some little thing. If they both liked each other, she thought, wouldn't it be wonderful if they got together! They really would make a splendid couple, but at the moment they both seemed shy of each other.

Tansy showed Katy the drawing of the Howard mansion.

"Why, that is it exactly!" Katy exclaimed. "That's the big house. Did you draw this?"

"Yes, it's a thank you for Tansy."

"Well Tansy, it's about time you went into the house. You keep making excuses. Remember, your father and mother had a happy time there, even though it was for such a short time. And many generations of Howards sang and danced there. It is the most beautiful house inside."

"Will you come with me, Katy, and maybe you as well, Soldier? I don't know why, but the house scares me."

So it was decided that the next day the three of them would go inside.

"But remember this," Tansy warned. "We must be careful. There still could be something of the plague there."

The next day when they entered the house Tansy was surprised at how bright the hallway was. It was because at the top of a wide stairway there was a large stained glass window. Doors opened each side of the hall. One led them into a large library. Books on huge shelves from floor to ceiling covered every wall.

Big armchairs and couches covered in red velvet had at one time been beautiful but now were torn and dirty. They went from room to room. Tansy could imagine how beautiful it must have been. They climbed the wide staircase. Rooms went each side of it along long corridors. Tansy opened the first door at the top of the stair. She gasped. It was huge.

"Yes," Katy said at her elbow. "This is the ballroom. Isn't it splendid?"

Indeed it was. The oak floor still looked after twenty years as if it had been newly polished. Round the walls beautiful tapestries were still as bright in their reds and blues. A large chandelier hung each side of the ballroom, twinkling in the light from the windows. One of the rooms on the far side from the ballroom she guessed was her mother and father's. The furniture was of the palest wood. "Ash," Soldier said.

A huge double bed dominated the room. It was draped from the ceiling in soft blue and gold curtains. A Persian carpet covered the floor picking out the blue and gold of the bed hangings.

A large dressing table was filled with silver tipped bottles. Tansy opened one. The perfume was still as strong.

"It's Jasmine," Katy said. "That was one of your mother's favourite perfumes."

Tansy had a fleeting moment of something near her. She felt so close to her mother

"Katy, you realise that all this will have to go." She waved her hand at the curtains, the bed, the carpets. "And I mean from every room. It's possible that the rats have been in here. Their fleas could be anywhere. All the soft furnishings must be destroyed. I will try to save the tapestries. If I can make something up with herbs they can maybe be taken down and laid out on the lawn and dusted.

"Soldier, could you help with all this? The women who cleared out the cottages said they would be prepared to do some more work for me. But they must come prepared. Hands and arms must be covered. Shawls on their heads. We will need a number of carts to take away the lots for burning."

CHAPTER 36

IT seemed to Tansy the next day that half the village women had turned up. If it weren't so sad it would have been laughable. They were dressed up in all sorts of things to cover them. One or two had even borrowed their husbands' trousers.

Soldier was there giving out instructions. The women paid attention. Some of them had had someone close die with the plague and knew the horror of it.

One by one the carts were loaded up, taken to one of the fields and burnt. This went on all day, the carts back and forward. On one of them Tansy saw the drapes of her parents' bed. She felt like crying then.

Soldier caught one of the village women trying to hide a feather eiderdown. It was a beautiful one covered in pink satin, but Soldier was having none of it. The woman was sent home. It was an example to the rest. They were all there to earn a few shillings. That woman went home with nothing.

Tansy felt so sorry for them all. Here they were burning things that they could never in their lifetime afford.

The livestock sales were on in Trent that afternoon. The Howard estate got the highest prices for their livestock for the first time in many years. At last the estate was bringing in much needed money.

Tansy and Katy celebrated that night. They sat at the usual place at the kitchen table with a bottle of wine. Maybe it was because of the wine that Tansy got the courage to ask Katy if she had feelings for Soldier.

Katy blushed scarlet.

"Oh Tansy, do you think I am an old fool? Yes, I do have feelings for him. He is a good kind man. I think that maybe he feels the same about me but nothing has been said."

Tansy hugged her. "I think you make a wonderful couple. I am so fond of you both. I hope things work out for you."

A few days later Tansy was busy working in the dairy. Two of the village women were helping her, scrubbing the shelves that Soldier had put up. Because of the amount of milk that was now coming in, butter and cheese would be made there and sold at the market every week. The two women were good clean workers. Tansy asked them if they would like to be taken on as dairymaids.

They were both over the moon with thanks. "You won't regret it. We will work hard for you."

Tansy felt a great deal of satisfaction herself. They were the first workers she had taken on herself.

She looked up at the big house as she left the dairy. Maybe she would get used to living there. As she turned away something made her turn and look back at the house. High up at the top of the house where the servants' quarters were a man was standing looking down. He turned and went inside. It all took place in a quick second. Tansy was troubled. Was it her imagination? Maybe it was just a shadow. She never mentioned it to anyone and forgot about it because when she went back to Katy's, Soldier and Katy met her.

Soldier said, putting his arm round Katy, "This wonderful lady has promised to marry me. We will just have a quiet wedding in the estate church if you don't mind. The last wedding there was your mother and father."

"Oh, I think that's such a wonderful idea," Tansy said.

And at the back of her mind she thought, 'I don't suppose I will ever marry. There or anywhere else.'

Sir Edward called to see Tansy.

"Now, who has been a naughty young lady?"

Tansy, busy in the dairy, was quite sharp with him. "What do you mean, Sir Edward?"

"Well, remember the night you sang at my musical evening an old couple were moved to tears when you sang?"

"Oh yes," Tansy said. "I remember them. A lovely couple."

"Well, Tansy, that lovely couple happen to be Lord and Lady Kilmore, one of the wealthiest people in England. And that 'old couple' as you call them gave you an invite to the biggest event of the year in London. I believe that royalty are to be among the guests and you, Lady Tansy Howard, did not even bother to reply. The invites to the big occasion always go out weeks in advance."

"But Sir Edward, I did not receive an invitation," Tansy started to say. Then she remembered the card they gave her. She had been so upset that night when Eva said she was getting engaged to Tom that she hadn't looked at the card. She had just wanted to get away. She had stuck it in her little silver bag.

"Well, my dear," Sir Edward said. "It's not for another two weeks. You can still reply—if you want to go, that is."

"What am I going to do?' Tansy moaned to Katy. "I know that you still have some lovely dresses in your trunk but I would need to wear something grand. Imagine, Katy, royalty might be there."

Soldier came in. He gave Katy a quick hug. "Why the long faces, you two?"

Katy explained to him about Tansy's invitation.

"Well Tansy, you have a lot of valuable pictures up in the big house. Why don't you sell one?"

"Why do you think they are valuable, Soldier? To me they just looked old and full of dust."

"We will soon find out. Come on up to the house."

They went as before from room to room but now it was the pictures they were looking at. Now and then Soldier gave a whistle.

"My God, Tansy. If I am right, you have got a fortune here."

Tansy looked at them more carefully. Yes, there was something wonderful about them.

"We will have to get help to get them down. We could store them in the barn beside the tapestries. Some of the portraits I can recognise. There is a look of my father in a lot of them. You pick one that you like, Soldier, and we will take it to London. Maybe I *will* get that dress."

Katy had been prowling around. Tansy had forgotten that she knew the house better than she did. "Come and look at this!" she shouted. She was coming out of one of the rooms near the kitchen. She had opened up huge cupboard doors inside.

They were full from floor to ceiling with silver candelabras, cutlery, everything needed to put on a display of wealth in the dining room.

"I remember it all," Katy said. "It was last used at your mother and father's wedding. Over a hundred guests attended. Ralph had no interest in looking in cupboards otherwise I'm sure he would have used it for money for his gambling."

Tansy was speechless. "To think that all this money was sitting here and I have been counting every single penny."

"Right," Soldier said. "All this will have to be packed away in trunks and locked. Since the plague and fire in London a lot of pretty rough people have been roaming the country. We have been lucky so far. I'll get the village men up to pack away all this safely before we go to London."

"When we go to London, Katy, and if we get enough money for the picture, why don't I buy your wedding outfit?"

"Oh Tansy, how kind you are! But we better wait and see what happens."

"Tell me, Katy. What is Soldier's real name?"

Katy laughed. "Don't tell me you don't know his name after all the time he has been here? Well, Tansy, his name is James Grant, ex-army, only son of James Grant Senior and Mrs Grant. James' father was an army man for many years in India and James was born in India and lived there until he came home to school in England. His parents are both dead. Hold on, he gave me loads of sketches. I'll go and fetch them."

They both looked through the sketches, an artist's impressions that depicted Soldier's parents. His father was so like him, his mother a small delicate looking woman.

Soldier came in. "Oh, looking at my past, I see!" He picked up the sketch of his mother. "I heard you saying she looked delicate. Well, looks deceive. She was as tough as old boots. My father was a Colonel commanding a regiment but my mother bossed him around. They were very happy together. So you will be Mrs James Grant in a few weeks." Katy blushed. Tansy saw such happiness in her face.

The next day they set off for London, Soldier carrying the large painting carefully wrapped in canvas. It was a painting done in oils. The richness of the colours of a beautiful landscape. Tansy, knowing nothing about paintings, was awed by it.

"I think you made such a good choice, Soldier."

"Well, I hope so, but if not we can go back and pick another one. It's like an Aladdin's cave back there."

When they arrived Soldier led the way to the more prosperous part of London where the best shops and galleries were. When they entered the first gallery, Soldier, not hanging about, asked to see whoever was in charge of buying pictures. The man he asked looked at him disdainfully. "I'm afraid you need to make an appointment Sir." Soldier took a step towards him until he was nearly nose-to-nose with him.

"I want you to take us to him now!" he bellowed in his loud drill voice.

The man, looking scared, said, "Right away Sir, right away."

Katy said afterwards the poor man thought he was dealing with a madman.

They followed him up two or three flights of stairs. The man knocked on the door. A gruff voice shouted, "Enter!"

"These people want to see you Sir. He appears to have a picture to let you see."

"Very well Jones. Off you go. No need for you to wait."

Tansy looked at the man behind a large desk. Why, she thought to herself, he looks really homely to hold such a grand position.

He looked at Soldier. "Well now, let's see what you have here."

"Well Sir, the picture belongs to this lady, Lady Tansy Howard of the Howard estate in Trent. And this is her friend Katy who I am going to marry shortly."

The man came from behind the desk. He shook hands with them all. "And you Sir, your name?"

"James Grant," Soldier said.

"Ex-army I believe. Am I correct?"

"Yes Sir, quite correct," Soldier said.

"I am Nigel Haldane. I am sorry about the interrogation, but it's not often I get such unexpected visitors." He smiled. "Now let's all sit down and have tea and we can discuss this picture you are carrying."

Over tea he talked to Tansy about the estate. "You are very young to have such responsibility."

Soldier got up, impatient to get on with showing the picture. He opened up the canvas and lent the picture against the desk. He heard a crash and turned round. Nigel Haldane had jumped up, scattering the tea things in his excitement.

"How did you come by it? I have one downstairs by the same artist. I have heard about this one. Never thought it would ever appear. Come, tell me the story about where it's been."

So Tansy told him the whole story, also telling him about the other paintings.

"I thought that maybe you could send someone to value them."

He was beside himself with excitement. "Of course. I hope you have them somewhere safe. Now I can't tell you the value of this painting immediately. Could you come back tomorrow?"

He saw the look of disappointment on Tansy's face. "Oh, you were maybe wanting to have a shopping spree. Now if I gave you a receipt for the painting and maybe three thousand pounds, would that help you?"

They all gasped. Tansy, collecting herself, said, "Yes Mr Haldane, that will do nicely. We can come back tomorrow morning."

For Tansy the next day was like a dream. Soldier went off to see his friends leaving Katy and Tansy to visit the shops looking for the all-important dress.

That morning the three of them had visited the gallery. They had a meeting with Nigel Haldane. Tansy still couldn't believe what he told them. For the honour of displaying the painting in the gallery they would pay ten thousand pounds. He advised Tansy to talk it over with her lawyer and get it all done legally. He also suggested that all the remaining paintings should be valued and kept safe till they were returned to the house or sold.

Tansy smiled to herself. Here she was being told about all that money and all she was interested in was buying a dress.

She remembered the shop that Gran-Mere had taken her to, to buy the dress for her sixteenth birthday. When they walked into the shop it was exactly the same and Tansy could swear that it was the same woman who met them.

CHAPTER 37

THEY sat and watched as dress after dress was displayed to them but Tansy saw nothing she liked.

"Is this dress for a special occasion?"

"Yes, very special. It's a party at Lord and Lady Kilmore's."

The woman waved her hand. An assistant appeared immediately. The woman whispered to her and the assistant came back with a dress over her arm. It was red velvet, the colour of claret wine.

"It's absolutely beautiful," both Tansy and Katy agreed. "The velvet is so soft."

"I think it's your size," the saleswoman said. "Would you like to try it on?"

When Tansy emerged from the fitting room, Katy said, "Oh Tansy, that's the dress for you."

Even the hardened saleswoman looked genuinely impressed. "It certainly is your dress, my dear."

Tansy looked at herself in the long mirror. The dress really *was* beautiful. It seemed to flow from her bare shoulders to a tiny v-shaped waist, then a very small bustle brought it to a train that swept out behind. The saleswoman was getting quite excited.

"Now, no jewellery. Just a string of pearls and maybe a pearl ornament for your hair. Black velvet slippers and a black velvet evening bag. I think we have got just the things next door."

The assistant came back with matching bag and shoes and also a long black lace stole that she would remove when she went inside.

"You must not cover up the lovely lines of the dress," she said.

Tansy, thrilled to bits, asked for them to be packed and it was only then she decided to ask the cost. When she was told that it was nearly one thousand pounds she was ready to tell the women that she didn't want them; but Katy spoke up: "I think that's just fine Tansy, don't you?"

Tansy turned to the saleswoman. "This is my friend Katy. She is getting married soon so we will need an outfit for her. I mean, everything. Nice underwear, nightwear, the lot." She turned to Katy. "This will be my wedding present to you."

Katy chose a pale lilac dress and a matching three quarter length coat. She also bought her a silver fox stole. "In case you catch a chill," Tansy grinned at her. So they both left the shop feeling guilty at what was spent but never in their lives had they had such a good time.

Soldier met them later in the day. "Would you mind, Tansy, if I stayed here another day? There is going to be a bit of an army reunion."

"What a good idea, Soldier. In fact, Katy, why don't we stay till after the party? It's only two days away. It would be such a nuisance going back and forward to Trent. Besides, I still have to see the lawyers about the paintings." So it was decided.

The time passed quickly and it was the night of the party.

"Will you be all right, Katy?"

"Yes, I'll be just fine. Soldier will be here to look after me."

Tansy got dressed. "Now Katy, what do you think?" she asked as she twirled round.

"I think you look so much like your mother that I could cry. I loved her. She was like a sister to me, and you, my beautiful Tansy, are like a daughter."

The coach arrived. Some of the hotel guests stopped to stare at the beautiful young woman in the red velvet dress.

She arrived at the huge mansion house. A footman opened the door of the coach and led her into the house.

It reminded her a bit of Sir Edward's house but on a much grander scale. Another footman took her stole and led her upstairs. 'I could get lost in here,' Tansy thought. He opened the door that led to the ballroom. "Lady Tansy Howard!" he announced. To Tansy the whole large room seemed to be glittering, four large chandeliers shedding sparkling lights. The ballroom doors opened into the dining room, the tables shining with silver and crystal.

The band was playing softly. No one was dancing. There was an air of expectancy in the room. Someone whispered to her: "His Royal Highness King Charles is expected." She picked a glass of wine from a waiter and looked around. Then her eyes were drawn like a magnet across the room. A tall man with reddish brown hair was standing with his back to her. It was as if he felt her eyes on his back. He turned round. It was Tom.

His face broke into the smile she loved so much. He crossed the room to her.

"Gosh Tansy, you are so beautiful." He held her hand. "I was going to Trent tomorrow to see you. We have got so much to talk about."

The band struck up the National Anthem. King Charles entered the room. The guests seemed to have formed two lines and the King, led by Lord Kilmore, was being introduced to some of the guests.

They stopped in front of Tansy and Tom. Lord Kilmore introduced them.

"So you are the nightingale," he said to Tansy. "Maybe you will sing tonight?"

"I would be honoured Sir," she said.

He spoke to Tom. "I visited your estate many years ago. A wonderful part of Scotland."

He moved on. Tansy felt the giggles coming on. Tom pinched her arm. It felt like the old days when they were boy and girl in Redburn.

"Sorry," Tansy said. "It was just nerves. Why are you keeping on staring at me Tom? Have I got a smut on my face?"

"No Tansy, you have the most beautiful face. I just like looking at it."

A dance started playing and everyone started to dance.

"Will you do me the honour of this dance, Lady Tansy?" Tom asked.

"You may, Sir Tom."

And that's the way it continued most of the evening, each one trying not to show their feelings.

The large supper had ended, everyone drifting back into the ballroom.

Lord Kilmore approached Tansy.

"Will you sing, Tansy? His Royal Highness would love to hear you."

"Yes, of course." She followed Lord Kilmore to where the band was set up. She curtsied to the King. He acknowledged her with a smile.

Tansy thought her first impression of him of being quite a plain man was wrong. He was anything but. There was something magnetic about him that drew people to him. It certainly wasn't his looks. He wasn't very tall. He had a rather long nose. His black curled wig falling to his shoulders would have looked ridiculous on anyone else, but it seemed to suit him.

CHAPTER 38

TANSY started to sing 'The Water is Wide.'
She looked across the large room to where Tom was standing and
when she sang the verse—

> And neither have I wings to fly
> Give me a boat that will carry two
> And both shall row my love and I

—it was as if no one else was in the room but herself and Tom, and she
was sending him a message. She finished off singing the old favourite,
'Nut Brown Maiden.' Once again, when she had finished, there was
silence. Then the applause rose, going on and on.

His Royal Highness spoke to her. "You have been gifted with one of
the most beautiful voices I have ever heard. It will bring pleasure to
many people."

Tansy curtsied to him and thanked him but she couldn't wait to get
away to find Tom. He was standing by the door leading into the garden.

He put out his hand and led her outside. They just stood there, saying nothing.

Then Tom spoke. "What are we going to do, Tansy? You do know that I love you? But you are with Ian, my best friend."

Tansy drew back. "What do you mean I am with Ian? What nonsense. Ian is also my best friend."

"But Eva told me that you and Ian would marry."

Tansy laughed. "Eva told me that she was getting engaged to you and I saw you kissing her when we lived at Dr Brown's."

"I remember that day. You were so cold to me. I wasn't kissing her—she was kissing *me*. I bet she saw you watching and did it out of malice. Oh Tansy, how foolish we have been! I love you so much. What are we to do? We both have commitments."

Tansy kissed him. "Our love will find a way. I can hear Gran-Mere saying that! We have such a lot to talk about, Tom. Do you know that Katy and Soldier are getting married? And you must come to Trent and see all that has happened on the estate. And I must tell you about all the pictures."

"Hold on Tansy," Tom was laughing. "You are just like an excited little girl."

She put her arms round his neck. "A very happy girl," she said.

The four of them set off for Trent the next day. They were all so happy. As they entered Trent they saw black smoke billowing up to the sky.

"Some burning going on," Soldier remarked.

As they drew nearer they saw tongues of fire among the smoke.

Soldier, leaning out of the coach, shouted, "My God, it's the big house!" They rushed up. It was terrifying to watch. Flames were coming out of every window. As they looked a man came out to one of the window ledges. The man was yelling: "This is what you get for what happened to my brother! The old witch cursed us. We should have killed her. He was dying like a dog in the road outside the witch's house!" His voice was fading. The sound of the fire was like a huge wind. The man deliberately turned and walked back into the fire.

There was nothing anyone could do to save the man or the house. It burnt for three days. Tansy remembered the man. She had caught a glimpse of him on the top of the house days before. He must have been one of Ralph's helpers, to do evil along with his brother.

There was a great deal of sadness especially among the older generation. It was the loss of a house that their forbearers had known for many generations.

Though Tansy had never lived in it she felt sad at its loss. It had been the Howards' pride and joy for many generations.

Tom put his arms round Tansy. "Don't be too upset. We will all help to get it rebuilt."

"But it won't be the same, Tom. There is nothing left. Even the walls had to be knocked down. They were too unsafe to leave. Thank goodness the outbuildings are fine and the estate can go on as usual."

They walked back to Katy's.

Tom stopped walking. He put his hand under Tansy's chin and looked into her eyes.

"My darling Tansy, will you marry me?"

"Soon, very soon. We have wasted so much precious time together."

When they arrived at Katy's both she and Soldier laughed. "We were both wondering when you two would get on with it. And while we waited for you two to decide Soldier and I came up with an idea that might help you both. That's of course if you both agree." Katy continued: "Soldier and I will of course be staying here but we could with maybe the help of Bob White and Nancy, run both estates. Bob and Nancy could move into one of the cottages. You would be free, Tansy, to go with your husband to Scotland." Here she laughed. "Unless you change your mind about marrying Tom."

Tom and Tansy sat speechless. They were quiet for such a while that Katy and Soldier looked worriedly at each other. Had they been too forward with their suggestions?

Tom leaped across the room and whirled Katy round and round. "I think that you and Soldier are wonderful. What a great idea!" He turned to Tansy. "Don't you think so, Tansy?" Then he noticed that Tansy had tears streaming down her cheeks. "Gosh Tansy, what's wrong?"

"Oh Tom, I am so happy. What great friends we have."

It took a few more days to get things sorted out. The White family were delighted to move into one of the cottages. They would have it for life.

Tansy and Katy made another trip to London, this time to buy Tansy's wedding dress. It had to be something special because the wedding portrait would be hanging in Baldune House and maybe another in a rebuilt house here on the estate.

This time Tansy chose something simple but elegant in white satin with a long train. The veil was Gran-Mere's. On her head she wore a small hooped diamond tiara.

They were married in the little estate church. Tansy shed a tear for her mother and father who had had such a short time together.

Sir Edward as a wedding present to them gave them the wedding reception in his home. Two days later they attended Katy and Soldier's wedding. The barn at Tansy's was once again used for a big event, but this time there was no Ralph to spoil Katy's happiness.

Before Tom and Tansy left for Scotland Soldier presented them with the picture he had painted of the big house. It was correct in every detail. He even had drawn plans of what it looked like inside

"You see, Tansy. Some day you can have it back." Tansy hugged him, too overcome to speak.

Tansy and Tom followed almost in the same footsteps as Ian and Gran-Mere, travelling into the heart of the Highlands. Tansy clutched Tom's hand. "It's all so beautiful, Tom. I could cry."

They stopped at the same narrow gorge that Ian and Gran-Mere had, looking down the valley towards their future home.

Everything was so quiet and peaceful.

"Look, Tansy, you are privileged. Up there," he pointed. A golden eagle seemed to be just hovering before, in one flash of its huge wings, it flew off.

Loch Munda and all the village cottages were still exactly as Gran-Mere had described. "She would have been so happy if she knew that we were here in the place she loved. But you know, Tom, I get the feeling that she has been guiding us both to this very day."

The villagers led them to the boat on the shore, the village bell singing out. In answer across Loch Munda from Baldune House came the sound of bagpipes playing a welcome to them.

♣

The boys rode straight up to the front door and threw the horses' reins to the stable boy.

"Make sure you give them a good rub down. They have been put through their paces today."

A girl came to the door. "You boys will be in trouble if dad sees you riding up to the door. You know you should go straight to the stables?"

"Sorry sis," the taller of the boys said. He was a good-looking boy with reddish brown hair and bright blue eyes. The other boy, dark haired with dark eyes, grinned at the girl in the doorway.

"Keep your hair on, Maria. We won't do it again, but we are in a hurry to go to the fête in the village. Are you coming with us, Maria?"

Maria tossed her long fair hair, her blue eyes flashing. "I certainly don't want to go with you, James Grant. You are always tormenting me and playing tricks on me." She drew herself up. "I am fourteen. It's time you treated me like a lady."

Edward Moncrieff laughed. "Come on sis, relax. Come with us, it will be fun. I'll look after you. I'm two years older than you, remember."

The boys raced up the wide staircase, nearly knocking down the two women on their way down

"Really!" the fair-haired woman said. "They get wilder every time we come back here."

"Blame that son of mine, Tansy. James is so happy when Edward is here. They are closer than brothers. I still can't believe, Tansy, that James is my son. He came to Soldier and me like a miracle. I never thought it would happen."

Tansy hugged her. "Katy, you and Soldier make the most wonderful parents."

Tansy looked around. "Talking of miracles, Katy, just *look* at this house! Isn't it splendid? Who would have thought it could ever happen when we looked at the ashes of it that day."

"I do wish you could stay here for longer periods, Tansy. I know that Baldune is close to your heart."

"Well Katy, who knows. Gran-Mere taught me that life with its many twists and turns holds many surprises. No one knows what is ahead."

Tansy, thinking back to the time of the terrible plague and the thousands who had lost their lives, took Katy's arm.

"Come on now, Katy. Let's just count our blessings, which are many, and live each day as it comes."

The End.

About the Author

BORN in Ballachulish, Argyllshire in 1934. Married, had five children; divorced after 25 years. When the children grew up and married, worked in hotels. Had a snack van in Glencoe, selling hamburgers. Worked at Sullen Voe in the Shetlands at the oil terminal. Went back to school at 40, obtaining English O-level with General Studies. Now travels over Europe; visited Egypt, Kenya. Her big love is gardening.

www.ingramcontent.com/pod-product-compliance
Lightning Source LLC
Chambersburg PA
CBHW020616250626
47154CB00004B/1531